Dear OwlCrate Jr. Reader,

what interesting things did you experience today? I ask because my inspiration for this book began to emerge when I was around your age. My teacher collected beautiful magazine covers that we used to spark story ideas. Many years later, I wondered what would happen if those stories we wrote came true. That's what happens to J.R. Silver, much to her surprise!

To me, stories are magical—even if their magic isn't obvious. So I hope you'll keep your eyes and ears open because a spark of an idea is coming to you.

Enjoy reading this OwlCrate Jr. signed first edition,

Melissa Dassori

J.R. SILVER WRITES HER WORLD

J.R. SILVER WRITES HER WORLD

MELISSA DASSORI

WITH ILLUSTRATIONS BY CHELEN ÉCIJA

Christy Ottaviano Books

LITTLE, BROWN AND COMPANY

New York Boston

Text copyright © 2022 by Melissa Dassori
Illustrations copyright © 2022 by Chelen Écija

Cover art copyright © 2022 by Chelen Écija. Book pattern © MOHYTYCH YUSTYNA/Shutterstock.com; doodle line © WinWin artlab/Shutterstock.com; pen vector © ddok/Shutterstock.com. Cover design by Jenny Kimura. Cover copyright © 2022 by Hachette Book Group, Inc.

Christy Ottaviano Books
Hachette Book Group
1290 Avenue of the Americas, New York, NY 10104
Visit us at LBYR.com

First Edition: July 2022

Christy Ottaviano Books is an imprint of Little, Brown and Company. The Christy Ottaviano Books name and logo are trademarks of Hachette Book Group, Inc.

The publisher is not responsible for websites (or their content) that are not owned by the publisher.

Notebook vector © Progdiz/Shutterstock.com. Pen vector © ddok/Shutterstock.com.

Library of Congress Cataloging-in-Publication Data
Names: Dassori, Melissa, author. | Écija, Chelen, illustrator.
Title: J.R. Silver writes her world / Melissa Dassori ; with illustrations by Chelen Écija.
Description: First edition. | New York : Little, Brown and Company, 2022. |
Audience: Ages 8–12 | Summary: J.R. struggles to navigate the torments of middle school, made thornier by her secret power to write wishes into existence.
Identifiers: LCCN 2021033586 | ISBN 9780316331456 (hardcover) |
ISBN 9780316331678 (ebook)
Subjects: CYAC: Ability—Fiction. | Wishes—Fiction. |
Middle schools—Fiction. | Schools—Fiction. | LCGFT: Novels.
Classification: LCC PZ7.1.D33554 Jr 2022 | DDC [Fic]—dc23
LC record available at https://lccn.loc.gov/2021033586

ISBNs: 978-0-316-33145-6 (hardcover), 978-0-316-33167-8 (ebook)

Printed in the United States of America

LSC-C

Printing 1, 2022

For Fred

It is not often that someone comes along
who is a true friend and a good writer.
—E. B. White, *Charlotte's Web*

J.R.
SILVER
WRITES HER
WORLD

Chapter 1

"THAT ONE," SAID VIOLET AS she stepped so close to the railing that a blue-suited guard waved her back. "Definitely that one."

Violet spread her fingers and stretched her arms above her head in an exaggerated yawn that she turned into a grin. The source of her satisfaction was a three-hundred-year-old canopied bed framed by blue silk curtains. J.R. wouldn't have deemed it the best place to sleep in the Metropolitan Museum of Art, but she was relieved by her friend's enthusiasm. Violet had been moping around all morning, which was no way to spend the last Friday of summer before the start of sixth grade.

When it came to hunting for beds at the Met, J.R. and Violet were experts. They had played their own version of *From the Mixed-Up Files of Mrs. Basil E. Frankweiler* more times than either could remember. Like the stars of the book, who run away from home and hide out in New York City's most famous museum, the girls had identified the best beds to sleep

in and the fanciest fountains for bathing. They knew where to find an old American card table so they could play gin rummy, a gold-covered armoire that would hide their clothes, and a blue china tea set from which to "take refreshment," which they both liked to say in snooty British accents. They had even practiced squatting over imaginary chamber pots.

Violet leaned over the railing for one more look, accidentally unleashing her long brown curls and making her earrings swing. The blue circles with ornate white Ms on them were styled after the metal buttons the Met once used as admission tickets. J.R. gave the pair to Violet for her tenth birthday, and she planned to get some herself when she turned thirteen and could get her ears pierced. Violet delicately brushed her hair behind her shoulders. "What about you?" she asked. "The usual?"

To hear Violet say "the usual" made J.R. feel boring, but she did have a usual pick. Her favorite bed was in the Haverhill Room, a nineteenth-century New England bedroom in the museum's American Wing. It was a lot simpler than the re-created French palace where they were standing, but it still had its own four-poster bed, just one that was covered in plain white cotton instead of fancy blue silk.

As they passed by a series of medieval statues, Violet pulled out her phone for the millionth time that morning. She was carrying an impractically small purse, so to check her texts she had to squeeze the phone out past the zipper, tempting it to burst.

The only thing J.R. had with her was a pack of tissues.

Allergy season was not her friend. "I still can't believe your parents got you a phone," she said.

"Yours really won't budge?" Violet's eyes didn't leave her week-old device.

"They say I don't need one since my mom will pick me up."

Now J.R. had her friend's full attention. "First you couldn't go with me to Wachusett, and now your mom won't give up on pickup." Violet punched the word "up" both times. J.R. countered with a gentle elbow to the ribs. "I'm just saying," Violet added, making a "Who, me?" face.

"Just saying," J.R. repeated with enough humor to show goodwill.

"Well, one thing we do know is that Christmas wouldn't be Christmas without any presents," Violet riffed on the opening line from *Little Women*, another one of their favorite books. J.R. even liked to imagine that her parents had named her Josephine Rose after Louisa May Alcott's heroine, Josephine March. In truth, the Josephine in question was a great-aunt she'd never met.

Violet might have been onto something, though. December was probably the next best time to persuade J.R.'s parents to get her a phone. "Or Hanukkah," J.R. added, since her family celebrated both holidays.

"It's too bad your mom and dad are so strict these days."

It was too bad, but J.R.'s parents were always stricter than Violet's. Refusing to let her go to sleepaway camp or get a phone had been frustrating. Not letting her walk home alone was unbearable. Being a Walker was a privilege that students at Nic earned in sixth grade, and a very big deal. J.R. was determined to tackle this latest parental affront immediately. The challenge was how to do it. "What should I say to make them understand?"

Violet, lost in her phone, didn't answer.

J.R. was pretty sure that she was competing for attention with Ava Arls, the most popular girl in their grade. It made the whole situation worse.

A lot had changed over the summer. When J.R. and Violet learned that Ava was going to Violet's camp, neither of them was pleased. They wondered how she would survive the resident mascot, Sam the Snapping Turtle, and the frigid swims in Lake Wachusett, never mind Meatloaf Mondays. Somehow, though, Ava had more than survived. In fact, she thrived and played a bigger and bigger role in each letter J.R. received that summer. In early August, J.R. had been so distraught while reading about Violet and Ava's hike up Mount Washington that she walked straight into her downstairs neighbor, Mr. Richardson, and spilled his iced coffee all over his shirt. He had been so nice about it, asking if *she* was okay even though *he* was the one soaked and stained, that J.R. burst out crying and ran up to her apartment without even apologizing. Worse was that Mr. Richardson wasn't just any neighbor but the owner of her favorite store, June's Books, right on the Silvers' corner. The whole encounter was mortifying, and she hadn't gone into the shop ever since.

Watching Violet laugh at something Ava texted, J.R. found it hard to imagine what could be so amusing. She wanted to ask, but she couldn't figure out how without sounding nosy. "I hope we're in the same class again this year," she said instead, changing the subject entirely. There were two homerooms per grade at Nic, formally known as The Nichols School, and the girls had been together every year since kindergarten.

"Me too," said Violet. "Eventually they're going to separate us, though, so you have to be prepared."

Violet was right, but J.R. hoped this wasn't the year. She also wondered why Violet had said "you" instead of "we."

When the girls reached the huge glass atrium that marked the beginning of the American Wing, they stopped at the fountain by the entrance. Each pulled a penny from her pocket before they tapped their coins together for extra good luck, a ritual they had invented when they were little. Violet made a silent wish and threw her coin into the water. J.R. watched it sink before she closed her eyes and debated whether to ask for a golden retriever or a rescue dog. Either way, she was getting ahead of herself, since her parents had yet to agree to get a dog at all. When J.R. opened her eyes without making a decision, Violet was back on her phone.

"Isn't he adorable?" Violet flashed the screen to reveal a white Westie puppy. "Ava's parents had him waiting when she got home from camp."

Before J.R. was forced to muster excitement, Violet's mom unknowingly came to her rescue. "Fancy meeting you two here!" she called out in a faint lilt that J.R. always found soothing. J.R.'s mother stood beside her, an employee ID hanging on a red lanyard around her neck. Both women worked at the museum, Violet's mom curating photography exhibits and J.R.'s mother in the education office, where she had a boss who let her pick up J.R. from school and work at home in the afternoons. They had been friends forever, starting before their daughters were born.

"I thought we still had ten minutes?"

"You did, but I'm starving." Violet's mother shot her daughter a "time to put that away" look. "How many inches did you grow?" she asked as she pulled J.R. into a hug.

J.R. hadn't seen Violet or her mom all summer. She had assumed her friend would call as soon as she got home from camp, but two days later J.R. finally did the calling and was disappointed to find out that Violet wasn't free. The second time she proposed doing something, she didn't understand how Violet could be so booked up. By the third call, J.R. waited for Violet to suggest an activity, which she never did. Between unpacking, getting a haircut, and some cello lessons she needed to squeeze in, Violet was busy the whole week before she left again for Sri Lanka to visit her grandparents. It was J.R.'s mom who eventually arranged their morning at the Met.

"How did you know where we were?" J.R. asked.

"Simply a hunch." Her mom gestured toward a security guard in the corner. No wonder her parents hadn't been persuaded when she argued that walking home alone from Nic was just like walking around the museum.

"Since we're over here, can we see the Haverhill Room before we eat?" Violet asked.

J.R. suggested they skip it. She was having a hard time hiding the fact that she was in a bit of a funk. Maybe getting some food would make her feel better.

"Well, since J.R. doesn't mind, let's go up there another time. I just heard a grumble." Violet's mom clutched her stomach for effect.

Violet wrapped her arms around her own torso. "Let's eat, then. Immediately!"

J.R. had missed the Fernandos' banter. Violet had twin six-year-old brothers who never sat still, and her family talked *a lot*, but in a good way. Violet often claimed that J.R. was lucky to be an only child. J.R. wasn't so sure.

As the group headed toward the cafeteria, J.R.'s mom whispered something that made Violet's mom laugh.

Violet reached into her bag and checked her phone. Whatever she saw made her smile.

J.R. hung back and watched them all go. Then she closed her eyes and threw her penny into the fountain. She felt lucky that wishes had to stay secret in order to come true, since J.R. could never say hers out loud.

J.R. wished for her old best friend back.

Chapter 2

By the time school started on Monday, Ms. Kline had decorated her classroom ceiling to look like the night sky, and J.R. wondered how she had done it. She could have assembled black sheets of paper and pasted on the stars before she hung them all up. Or maybe she tacked up the paper and then added the constellations, like Michelangelo painting the Sistine Chapel. Both options made J.R. dizzy just to think about them. She spotted the Big Dipper and Cassiopeia, which looked like a stretched-out W. Then she found the North Star right between the two. Making eye contact with Violet, who had also been assigned to Ms. Kline's class, J.R. held up her hand and curled and uncurled her pinkie. Violet did the same. That was their signal they liked what they saw.

As a new teacher at Nic—so new, in fact, that she had only been hired in August—Ms. Kline was assigned room 602, which was bad news as far as her class was concerned. Students could use the elevators to reach the seventh and eighth floors, but below that they needed to walk. The climb was especially brutal at the start of the school year, and J.R. had to catch her breath while she looked for her assigned seat. When she found it, she picked up the list of class rules on top.

1. Be kind.
2. Late assignments will not be accepted.
3. Penmanship is important. Please write neatly.

"Stickler, eh?" Tommy Knowles commented as he sat down beside her.

"I still have a good feeling," J.R. answered optimistically, although things didn't seem as promising as when she first walked in.

In front of the whiteboard, Ms. Kline stood up noticeably straight. She wore black from head to toe and styled her dark-brown hair with a part down the middle and a low, tight bun. Her only pop of color was a faint line of blush across both cheeks. She had a vaguely Victorian air, kind of like a pale, porcelain doll, or maybe a porcelain doll in mourning. J.R.'s skin was downright pink by comparison.

Tommy, by even greater contrast, looked like he had just left the beach without wearing much sunscreen all summer. His nose was sunburned, and the orange and blue elastics on his new braces matched his Mets jersey. In the spring of fifth grade, Tommy had collected five jerseys to wear in line with the team's batting order, starting with the leadoff hitter each

11

Monday. Today, unfortunately, he had some breakfast stuck in his teeth, possibly a blueberry. J.R. wanted to tell him, but that would be awkward. So instead, she stayed silent and felt slightly disloyal. At least the blue matched the team colors.

J.R. scanned the room until she spotted Violet sitting next to Ava, which was just her luck. It looked like they had co-ordinated their outfits, too. Both wore purple tops, black leggings, and white sneakers, none of which J.R. had seen in Violet's closet before. Normally she put on baggy shorts and running shoes like J.R. was wearing. Whatever they were talking about was making the girls giggle. At the next group of desks, Ava's best friends, Adelaide and Aria, scowled in their direction.

Once everyone had found their seats, Ms. Kline said, "Excuse me," until she had the class's attention. "I'm Ms. Kline, and it's my pleasure to be your teacher this year. I've just moved to New York from the Northeast Kingdom."

"You moved from a fairy tale?" Curtis McBride's comment earned him a few guffaws.

"The Northeast Kingdom is at the very top of Vermont. It's quite a beautiful place, although I must say that I loved Miami, and the Mississippi Delta, and the San Juan Islands as well. Teaching in Hawaii was very special, too." Ms. Kline stared out the window wistfully, like the shingled water tower on the roof across the street might magically transform into a beach cabana. J.R. sneezed, bringing the teacher's attention back to the room. "Before we start, I'd like to get to know everyone. Please tell me one thing you particularly enjoyed doing this summer. Let's see," she said, scanning the class as Margaret's hand shot up from the seat opposite Tommy. "J.R., would you like to go first?"

"You mean Margaret," Tommy corrected, thinking Ms. Kline had mixed up his classmates.

"I know that's Margaret furiously waving her hand," said Ms. Kline. "But I'm asking J.R. to tell us one nice thing about her summer."

J.R. froze. She felt rusty and unprepared. Margaret didn't bother taking her hand down, which made the pressure worse. "I guess," she said, "I guess I really liked writing camp."

"You went to summer school?" Curtis called out.

J.R. fought the urge to glower in his direction. "It was a creative writing camp," she said matter-of-factly. "I went for three weeks at the public library."

"Writing camp sounds very interesting." J.R. took Ms. Kline's comment as a courtesy. The way she'd described it didn't sound that interesting, but elaborating would have meant talking about how she wanted to be a writer when she grew up, and that was more than she wanted to share on day one. "I look forward to hearing about it another time," Ms. Kline continued. "Now, Margaret, let's hear what's on your mind." Ms. Kline's raised eyebrows said this better be good.

Unsurprisingly, it wasn't. Margaret prattled on about a trip to Michigan with her softball team until Ms. Kline finally cut her off. Ava talked about climbing Mount Washington with

Violet, making it sound even better than Violet had in her letter. Curtis told the class about going to see the Yankees play the Red Sox with William, who was sitting next to him, and Matt Ghent, who was in the other sixth-grade class, unlike Matt Shah and Matt Malone, who were also in Ms. Kline's room. Tommy spent a week with his cousin on Long Island, which he described as "awesome" about ten times.

J.R. noticed that each of their stories revolved around friends.

When they finally made it through the whole class, Ms. Kline inhaled sharply. "Well then, that took quite a while." She blinked several times. "We've got a very full year ahead of us, so let's get started."

"Down to business," Tommy whispered, which earned him a withering look from Margaret. Tommy just rolled his eyes. Margaret was the worst.

The students watched while Ms. Kline pulled out three folders from the filing cabinets behind her desk. She opened them up and hung the stack of laminated *Gothamite* magazine covers across the whiteboard and along the room's window ledges. J.R. recognized the most recent one from the unsorted mail in the Silvers' living room. Her mom was a devoted subscriber, but the articles were usually too long for J.R.'s taste. Sometimes she scanned the write-ups of things to do in New York in the section called Gallivanting Around Gotham, which J.R. thought was clever.

Even if she didn't always look inside, J.R. studied the

Gothamite covers every week. The magazine put colorful illustrations on the front, not photographs, and there were no headlines or catchy phrases to mess up the image. In fact, the images weren't connected to the stories inside at all. It was like having a new work of art arrive constantly at her doorstep, or in the Silvers' mailbox to be precise. They even had titles that were listed in the magazine's table of contents.

Sometimes the covers were pretty. One of J.R.'s favorites was from the spring of fourth grade. It showed a cart full of flowers parked outside a florist's shop next to an entrance to the subway and a mound of melting snow, minus the black grime that would have actually coated the pile in New York City. The image was painted in tiny dots, and J.R.'s art class happened to be studying pointillism at the time.

Often the covers were funny, like the one that arrived close to Easter with a real-looking bird's nest filled with foil-covered eggs hatching yellow marshmallow chicks.

Other times, the covers weren't meant to be funny at all. One that J.R. remembered showed a group of old-fashioned Puritans rowing a rickety boat into New York Harbor. A sign on the stern said LIFEBOAT FULL. The Statue of Liberty was in the background, but instead of standing up tall she had her head bent down and her torch covering her eyes. It was one of the issues that J.R.'s mom had kept around for a really long time.

As J.R.'s classmates looked on—some blankly, a few enthusiastically, others with outright skepticism—Ms. Kline explained that for their first language arts unit, they were going to read memoirs. So for their first creative writing assignment, they would each pick one of the covers she had put out, most of which featured people on them, and write a short story based on the illustration. "You should let the images inspire you to take on a character and really become that person." Ms. Kline emphasized the last three words. "Consider it your chance to make the world about you."

This, J.R. thought, sounded interesting, especially since creative writing was her favorite part of school.

Ms. Kline continued introducing her lesson. "When you go home, I want you to make a list of five facts about your main character. You don't have to put them into your story, but they will help you get to know the person you're writing about. For example, Aria, can you tell me three distinctive things about Adelaide?"

Aria considered her answer. "Well, her favorite flowers are red roses. She likes to sing and she won the talent show at her camp this summer. And..." She paused. "And she sometimes eats chocolate pudding for breakfast!"

Adelaide, who had seemed to consider the first two facts compliments, blushed at the third.

"That's perfect. Thank you, Aria." Ms. Kline turned to the class. "So what can we infer about Adelaide from those facts? I'd say that if she likes red roses, maybe she's a romantic?" Curtis made kissing noises before Ms. Kline pressed her thumb and forefinger together and drew them across her

mouth. "What about winning her camp competition? What does that suggest?"

"It tells us she's talented!" Ava called out.

"That's right," Ms. Kline said, "although please raise your hand next time."

"I think it tells us she likes attention," Tommy whispered. Carlos nodded in agreement without looking up from the superhero he was doodling at his seat beside Margaret.

"And finally, the chocolate pudding?" Ms. Kline looked at the class expectantly. If she was disappointed by the resulting silence, she didn't show it. "It sounds to me like Adelaide has a sweet tooth, which is something I can relate to. I like to have one square of dark chocolate after dinner each night. So you see, if Aria had been writing about Adelaide, those facts would have helped her create a fully formed character, even if they didn't all make it into the story."

Ms. Kline went on to explain that they should use their imaginations rather than try to interpret the illustrations too literally, and that there would be plenty of covers to choose from. J.R. wished her teacher would stop talking so they could get started, but Ms. Kline wasn't done. "I got the idea for this assignment from my own sixth-grade teacher, Eleanor Mendell," she explained, "whose *Gothamite* collection dated back to World War I. Eleanor inherited many of them from *her* own sixth-grade teacher, who got them from?" Ms. Kline raised the pitch of her voice, soliciting an answer.

"Her sixth-grade teacher?" Margaret shouted.

"That's correct. When Eleanor retired, she passed along her magazines to me. If one of you is lucky, maybe you'll be next in line someday." Ms. Kline looked straight at J.R.

"Lucky you," Tommy murmured.

"One final note." By now J.R. could barely sit still. "I believe writing is meant to be private. You will write; I will read. Please write your assignments by hand, do not save them on a computer, and please do not share them with anyone else. Now, take your picks."

J.R. looked toward Violet, then gave another pinkie curl. This sounded like fun. She was pretty sure Violet curled back, but it was hard to tell since Violet left her hand on her lap.

The class rose from their desks and advanced toward the pictures. J.R. watched as Patrick quickly grabbed two covers. He held them against his rib cage with his elbow while he looked for a third. "What?" Patrick asked when Margaret gave him a look.

"Hoarder," she whispered.

Tommy didn't have any trouble making a decision. He went straight for the drawing of a young basketball player shooting a ball up over a defender while a row of scouts in suits whispered and watched. After baseball, football, and hockey, basketball was Tommy's fourth-favorite sport.

"Get it?" Tommy asked, pointing to the date at the top right corner. "It's from 1996. That's when the Lakers drafted Kobe straight out of high school. He was actually drafted by the Hornets and then traded. Bad move by the Hornets, eh?

High school players weren't really skipping college then, so it was a big deal."

"So you're going to write about how high school players shouldn't go pro?" J.R. asked, not sure she understood the point Tommy was making but knowing that *Gothamite* covers were usually commenting on something.

"I'm going to write about how awesome it would be to be that guy." Tommy pointed to the player who was about to sink his shot. That sounded more like it.

As J.R. kept looking, Kevin picked a cover from 1975. The colors had faded slightly, but it showed a redheaded man eating noodles straight from a white paper takeout carton while reading a newspaper with the headline "Americans Evacuate Embassy in Saigon." The man was sitting at a kitchen table with two fortune cookies beside him. The dome of the U.S. Capitol was visible outside his window. Kevin's dad had been a major in the Army, and when Curtis saw his selection he offered an exaggerated salute.

Violet took a picture of a girl playing the cello in what looked like her living room. Judging from the ages of the people watching, her audience included her parents, two sets of grandparents, and maybe some bored neighbors, as well as her brother. The little boy held up a toy helicopter in an unsuccessful attempt to get his father's attention, but the man was too busy filming the cellist to notice.

Violet played the cello, but her parents would never make her show off like that.

Before J.R. knew what happened, her options had dwindled to two, and neither was good. One, from the previous September, looked like a picture of the first day of school. A girl stood alone in the middle of a gym while a bunch of chatting parents headed for the door and her classmates gathered together in small groups. The girl did not look happy. The other cover was a picture of three men warming their hands over an oil drum in front of a wall covered in graffiti. It was from December 1981, and the sky was so dark that J.R. got cold just looking at it.

J.R. didn't feel like she had much of a choice. Even if she didn't love it, the lonely schoolgirl would have to do.

Chapter 3

THE LAST PERIOD OF THE first day was pretty much useless on account of the Walkers' excitement. J.R. doubted that any of them had absorbed Ms. Kline's opening lesson on Vikings, including the fact that the Norse explorers reached North America five hundred years before Christopher Columbus. Since J.R. was still a Greeter, which meant an adult would come greet her at pickup, she hadn't had any problem concentrating on the lesson. As far as she was concerned, school could have gone on forever. That would have been better than watching most of her classmates set out on their own while she waited for her mom.

At three o'clock, Ms. Kline gave up and sent the Busers down to the gym. Then the Walkers lined up by the door while the Greeters milled around until their teacher could escort them outside. Violet stood at the back of the line to keep J.R. company for as long as possible. Two spots ahead of her, Adelaide braided Ava's hair while Aria stood with her hand in her backpack, ready to document the moment as soon as they reached the street. At the front of the line, Curtis spun a football back and forth. He had been tossing it up and down until Ms. Kline made him stop.

"What if my mom talked to your mom?" Violet asked as the Walker line shrank.

"I don't think it would help. You just need to show my parents that it's safe, okay?"

Violet promised not to trip, get lost, or cross the street without looking, although she stopped short of swearing she wouldn't check her phone. By the time she finished her promise, she had reached the classroom door. Violet gave J.R. a gleeful smile tempered by a shoulder shrug. "Wish me luck," she said.

"Good luck!" J.R. obliged.

With the Walkers and Busers gone, Ms. Kline asked if the Greeters were ready.

"Wait one second," Nathalie cried out from the corner, where she was rooting around in the trash. "I think I threw out my retainer."

The Greeters let out a collective groan.

"Bummer, eh?" Tommy held a folded-up *New York Times* in one hand and a pen in the other. J.R. gave him a curious look. "I started doing the crossword puzzle with my grandma this summer," he explained. "I can only do some of Monday's, though, on my own. Then it gets too hard."

J.R. knew all about the daily puzzles from her dad,

who solved them religiously, and how they got harder over the course of the week. Sometimes she liked to help, but it had never occurred to her to try on her own and she was impressed. Crossword aside, J.R. wasn't sure if she was glad to see Tommy or embarrassed to be seen still standing in the room. "Bummer about the retainer, or about not being a Walker?"

"About not being Walkers, of course!"

Tommy and J.R. looked over at Nathalie, who had pulled the remains of a tuna fish sandwich out of the trash. It must have been Ms. Kline's lunch because students ate in the cafeteria. "Ugh," they said in unison.

"Jinx," said Tommy.

"How was it?" J.R.'s mom asked when they met up outside a few minutes later. As usual, she had a big canvas bag over her shoulder with a Met logo on the outside. It was bulging with papers.

J.R. sniffled as she looked up and down the street, but there was no sign of Violet. The only Walkers she saw from her class were Curtis, who was getting reprimanded by the head of the middle school for throwing a ball during pickup, and William, who was waiting for him. "Pretty good."

"And your teacher?" J.R.'s mom held out a tissue.

"Not sure yet," J.R. said, then took the tissue and blew her nose. If past experience was a guide, she would be battling the local ragweed for another two months. Any day now, her mom would probably break out a pack of Halloween-themed Kleenex, as if the holiday print made things better. "But she gave us a writing assignment that sounds good." Before J.R. could elaborate, her mom took a call.

J.R. went straight to her room when they got home. She sat down on top of her bed and pulled the string attached to the paper parrot that hung from the ceiling, sending its wings into motion. Without taking her eyes off the bird, she lay back and thought about the day. There was something odd about Ms. Kline. Her manner was so proper, and it was hard to say whether she was going to be fun, or strict, or both.

She also thought about Violet. J.R. had hoped that the start of school would return things to normal. Ava would pick up with Aria and Adelaide, and J.R. would get her friend back. But now that Violet was sitting with Ava, who of course was also a Walker, it felt like the reset might not come so easily. Maybe it wouldn't happen at all.

When the parrot's wings slowed, J.R. gave the string another tug and watched until they stopped entirely, which took a while. Without sitting up, she felt around for her backpack and extracted her *Gothamite* cover. The picture showed a bunch of families lined up in a gym like they were waiting to check in for something. Three boys chased one another in front of the bleachers, and some girls jumped rope on the opposite side of the room. A group of parents headed merrily for the door.

One girl stood in the middle and watched. The artist hadn't drawn her face in detail, but the way she stood all alone gave the impression she was sad, or maybe nervous. The problem was that J.R. wanted to write something happy, which was why she hadn't wanted the cover in the first place. Frustrated, she scribbled "left out?" and "scared?" in her notebook, which was part diary, part brainstorming grounds for her writing ideas. Lacking inspiration, J.R. started to wonder if Violet had stopped at Ava's house on her way home. She probably had.

J.R. put aside her homework and retrieved the *Mixed-Up Files* from her bookshelf. She had already read the book five times—six counting her mom's initial read-aloud—but she never got tired of Claudia and Jamie Kincaid's adventures hiding out at the Met while they try to determine whether a newly acquired statue called Angel had actually been carved by the famous Italian artist Michelangelo. There were so many things to love about the book, like how the siblings collect pennies while they take a bath in a fountain, how they memorize the guards' schedules so they know when to hide with their feet up on the toilets, and how they work together to solve the mystery of Angel's provenance. Just when J.R. got to the part where Claudia stashes her violin in a sarcophagus, her mom called out that dinner was ready. Closing the book, J.R. steeled herself to revisit the walking-home-alone discussion. If Claudia and Jamie were brave enough to run away, the least she could do was talk to her parents.

Through a window into their narrow kitchen, J.R. could

see her mom finishing something on the stove. Her dad put away a jar of spices before her mother grabbed it back. Her father was prone to rushing cleanup. "How was school?" he asked, coming over to plant a kiss on top of J.R.'s head.

"Good," she said, then grabbed a carrot stick from a bowl on the table. "But my new teacher's kind of strict." While she chewed, J.R. considered how best to describe Ms. Kline. "It's interesting because she's already worked in a lot of different places but she isn't very old, so she can't have been a teacher for long."

"Some people have wanderlust," her dad commented. "If she's good, I hope she stays longer at Nic."

J.R. liked the sound of the word "wanderlust" and made a mental note to use it in a story sometime. She didn't like the plate of salmon and broccoli that her mom put down in front of her. Focusing on the positive, she told her parents about Ms. Kline's *Gothamite* collection before her dad teasingly offered up her mother's overflowing pile of magazines.

"So I've been thinking about where we left things on the topic of me walking home after school." J.R. winced. Her shaky articulation—triggered by her desire to speak up before she chickened out—did not bode well for convincing anyone, never mind overprotective parents.

Her dad raised an eyebrow and licked a piece of broccoli from the corner of his mouth. For a compulsive cleaner, he wasn't particularly good with a napkin.

J.R. took a breath and mustered her best arguments for why it didn't make sense for her mom to leave work just to pick her up. After all, she always had to jump back on the computer as soon as they got home. Plus, Nic was practically around the corner from their apartment, or at least it was only six blocks away.

"Eleven years old seems really young to be walking around by yourself," her mom interjected. "And besides, I like our afternoons together."

Instead of pointing out how often her mother took calls from work on their way home, J.R. reminded her parents that she would be walking with Violet, who lived halfway between Nic and J.R.'s apartment if they took the most direct route. A slightly longer one went past Ava's building. J.R. wondered which way Violet planned to go, but that was beside the point.

"Your mother's happy to come get you, and we don't want you out on the street on your own," her dad said, eyeing J.R.'s untouched salmon. "Let's set this aside for now, and I'm not talking about your fish."

It felt impossible to muster the laugh that her dad was looking for. J.R. wasn't ready to leave it alone. She wanted to tell her parents they should trust her like Violet's parents trusted their daughter, but the words wouldn't come out. "Can we at least talk about it again over winter break?" she pleaded.

Her father agreed noncommittally.

J.R. ate half of her fish and most of her broccoli before her mom said she could be excused. Back in her room, she retrieved a pair of fuzzy purple slippers from her closet, then dug a stretchy Nic headband out of her top drawer and pulled it straight across her forehead. She knew that authors often had their own quirks when it came to writing routines, like Linda Sue Park always wrote at least two pages a day even if they were bad ones, and Jacqueline Wood- son had to write with her notebook turned sideways. Wearing the headband and slippers helped J.R. feel like a real writer, even if she looked ridiculous.

J.R. sat on her bed with her *Gothamite* cover and bit into an apple for dessert. She had two notebooks beside her: the one Ms. Kline had passed out for homework, and the one she liked to use for her own writing. It was red with a sticker on the cover that said "Just Write" and lined pages inside. J.R. doodled four daisies and a swan in the latter book while she ate her apple down to the core. As she chewed, she picked up her school notebook and made a list of facts about her main character, whom she decided to call Tess.

1. Short for her age (11)
2. Only child
3. Prefers gummy bears to chocolate

4. Prefers potato chips to gummy bears, most of the time
5. Doting grandmother lives nearby

"I believe an idea is sprouting," J.R. said to herself, accidentally swallowing a seed and chuckling at her own joke. If she couldn't walk home alone in real life, at least she could live vicariously through her story. J.R. started to write.

THE BIG DAY

For the last three months—since fifth grade ended, to be precise—I've been waiting for this day. Like everyone else in my sixth-grade class, now I can walk home on my own. No more Mom to bring me apple slices at 3:30, although that wasn't the worst routine in the world.

But now that the big day is here, I'm having second thoughts. What if I mess up the route (which I won't because I've done it a hundred times)? What if it rains and I forget my umbrella? (So what? It's only six blocks.) What if I forget my key? (Then I'd use the spare one under the mat, of course.)

I'm tempted to call out before Mom gets to the door. I could ask her to meet me like usual. I mean, do we really need to start this walking-home-alone thing on the very first day of school?

> But if I do that, I know I'll be disappointed.
> And a little embarrassed, too, so I swallow the
> lump in my throat. It's pretty small, but I can
> actually feel it go down.

J.R. wasn't writing particularly fast, but she felt like the
story was tumbling out as Tess got braver, like her pen was
moving her hand rather than the other way around.

> Deep breaths, I remind myself. Then I close
> my eyes, and imagine the route.
>
> - I'll head out of school and walk east to
>   Sisters' Deli, where I'll buy a snack, either
>   chips or gummy bears, depending on my
>   mood.
> - I'll go through three traffic lights and then
>   past the doorman who always says good
>   evening, even if it's the afternoon.
> - I'll pass six garbage cans if I walk on the
>   east side of the street and seven if I walk on
>   the west.
> - After I turn the corner on 91st Street, I'll
>   count twenty-six more steps until I reach
>   my building.
> - Then I'll use three different keys to get
>   in: the front door, the foyer, and the one

to our apartment, where for the first time in eleven years I'll have gotten myself home entirely on my own.

Piece of cake and easy as pie, as Grandma likes to say. (She likes lemon meringue, but I prefer blueberry.)

"Bye, Mom!" I say mostly to myself as I watch her leave the gym. My feet release from where they had been stuck to the floor. Maybe I'll even join the jump rope line.

J.R. tinkered with her story, giving Tess a light brown bob like her own and a green T-shirt inspired by the one hanging out of her hamper. When she was done, she tore out the pages along the perforated line and stapled them together. It felt like she had definitely followed Ms. Kline's instructions. J.R. was confident that she had brought Tess to life.

Chapter 4

THE SECOND DAY OF SCHOOL started a lot like the first, with no real surprises. After collecting their homework and taking back everyone's *Gothamite* cover, Ms. Kline taught the class about the constellations on the ceiling, since Viking sailors navigated by the stars. In gym, Curtis got in trouble for beaning Margaret in the nose during a fierce game of dodgeball; he was prone to throwing the ball a little too high at people he didn't like. In music, Mrs. Harris announced that the theme of the sixth grade's fall performance would be sea shanties. That was months away, so the shanties were hardly breaking news. Tommy wore a Giants T-shirt rather than a next-in-batting-order Mets jersey, so if J.R. was honest, that was *one* unexpected development of the day.

Just before dismissal, though, things got weird. First, Ms. Kline handed out books for their initial reading assignments. There were two to choose from—*El Deafo* and *Born a Crime*, which she brought in the adapted edition for kids.

"Um, this is a graphic novel," Adelaide said after Ms. Kline handed her a copy of *El Deafo*. Apparently, Adelaide hadn't looked closely before making her pick.

"It's a graphic memoir, actually," Margaret chimed in.

"And?" Ms. Kline asked.

"And we definitely haven't read comics in class before," Adelaide answered. "At Nic we read real books."

"*El Deafo* is certainly a real book," Ms. Kline said. "In fact, it's one of my favorites. But if you'd like to try the other option, you're welcome to. *Born a Crime* is Trevor Noah's story about growing up in South Africa as apartheid came to an end."

Adelaide looked tempted but decided to keep the book she had already. "At least it's short," she said.

Unsurprisingly, most of the boys chose Trevor Noah's book. The girls were more of a mix, with J.R. opting into the *El Deafo* camp. Ms. Kline's selections were definitely unusual— another sign that it was going to be an interesting year.

After everyone packed up to go home, things got even weirder.

"I know it's boring, but I feel like vanilla," Violet said from her spot near the front of the Walker line, which was more of a Walker mess. "What about you?" J.R. figured she must have missed the start of Violet's question while she had been looking out the window. There was supposed to be a thunderstorm, which meant that her soccer practice would probably be canceled. Before she could ask what Violet was talking about, her friend started shaking Ms. Kline's hand,

and J.R. turned reluctantly toward the Greeters. Nathalie was bent over the trash can again.

"Aren't you coming, J.R.?" Ms. Kline called out.

"But—"

"I need you to get going so I can help Nathalie with that retainer."

J.R. wasn't sure what was happening, but some misunderstanding was working in her favor. Trying to play it cool, she shook her teacher's hand and glanced quickly over her shoulder. Tommy was watching Nathalie and definitely not offering to help. In the hallway, Violet pulled her cello from the storage closet while Aria, Ava, and Adelaide waited. Rather than the bright bulging backpacks that J.R. and Violet had for their stuff, they each carried a thin canvas bag over one shoulder and had already stuck sunglasses onto their heads despite the cloudy weather.

"Ready?" Ava asked.

"Ready," the others answered.

J.R. couldn't tell if the question was meant for her as well until Violet looked over.

"Ready," J.R. said. She tried to sound like she meant it.

The five of them funneled into the stairway, which was a lot more chaotic when full of Walkers than when the Greeters and teachers descended. Out on the street, J.R. looked around, but her mom wasn't there. She was mostly relieved but also confused. Her mother never missed pickup, and J.R. wasn't supposed to be a Walker. What was going on?

"Interview?" Violet asked no one in particular as the girls headed uptown.

"What's interview?" Aria plunked a pacifier-shaped lollipop into her mouth. "Did you post it?" she asked after Adelaide snapped a picture. Adelaide flashed the phone's screen to show that the picture was now on Instagram.

"Interview is when one of us pretends to be a reporter, and one of us pretends to be a famous person being interviewed," Ava explained.

J.R. tried to catch Violet's eye, but Violet dodged her. They had made up the game in fifth grade. "You in?" Violet asked.

J.R. had to remind herself that Interview wasn't a secret or even something she had an exclusive claim to. "I'm in," she said. Then she decided to go one step further. "I'll be the first reporter."

"Cool," said Ava.

"And I'll be Milly Peace!" Adelaide volunteered.

Milly Peace was a sixteen-year-old singer who had started getting famous over the summer, but J.R. didn't know much more about her. Normally, the famous people she and Violet chose were authors, like Rick Riordan, or even fictional characters like Katniss Everdeen. Katniss was a bit of a sore spot. J.R.'s parents hadn't let her read the Hunger Games books until that summer. She suspected that they had only capitulated because they felt guilty about Wachusett.

Just as J.R. started with an easy question—"So, Milly, how old were you when you first knew you wanted to be a singer?"—the girls passed Jim, a homeless man who often sat in front of the grocery store two blocks north of school.

"Hi there," he said from his bench as the girls walked by. "What have we got this week?"

When Violet stopped to answer, Adelaide bumped into her. "I actually don't have a book going right now." Violet kind of looked embarrassed. Normally she was always reading something outside of school. "What about you?"

Jim held up a book with two men in long coats and brimmed hats walking down a winding street on the cover. It was night, and the old buildings looked like they were in Europe.

"Is it good?" Violet adjusted the weight of her cello as he passed her the book. Adelaide's and Aria's jaws dropped, requiring Aria to remove the pacifier pop from her mouth.

"It's excellent," Jim said while Violet skimmed the description inside. "It's got American actors, Russian spies, and France on the verge of war. Tell your dad he'd like it."

"Will do," Violet promised. She handed back the novel.

"You start school yet?"

A driver honked long and loud at the end of the block, and Violet waited for him to stop before she answered, "Yesterday."

"And how is it?"

Violet thought before answering. "I feel like it's going to be a good year." J.R. wondered exactly what her friend had in mind. Violet made small talk with Jim for another minute before she said goodbye and the girls continued their walk.

"Who was that?" Ava asked when they were out of earshot.

"Is he your friend?" Adelaide scrunched up her nose and fingered the sparkly silver "A" keychain hanging from her backpack.

"His name is Jim, and I wouldn't exactly call him a friend. He and my dad trade book recommendations sometimes," Violet explained. "They're both big readers."

"But where does he get books?" Aria asked.

"From the library on 96th Street," Violet said matter-of-factly.

"You do this, too?" Adelaide turned to J.R.

"She's afraid to talk to him," Violet interjected.

"I am not!" J.R. said, although it was a little bit true. Really, she was more uncomfortable than afraid. Violet never seemed bothered by Jim's missing front tooth, or the fact that it was kind of awkward to think about whether he had anything to eat for dinner when the girls were probably heading home for a starter snack and then a full meal. J.R. usually stood back a step when Violet talked to him, avoiding eye contact but trying to be friendly when it accidentally happened.

"I think that's nice," said Ava. "Maybe I'll get a library card, too."

As J.R. groaned silently, Adelaide turned in to Mathilda's Milkshakes, a tiny restaurant styled like a 1950s diner. Violet stashed her cello in the corner, then joined Ava at the counter. J.R. stood to the side as if dutifully guarding the instrument.

Ava ordered an Oreo shake for herself, vanilla for Violet, and coffee for both Aria and Adelaide. Everyone looked at

J.R., whose parents always steered her away from coffee ice cream on account of the caffeine. "I'm not really thirsty," she said.

"It's a milkshake!" Ava exclaimed. "You don't have to be thirsty."

J.R. hesitated. Then she decided to enjoy the afternoon while it lasted. "I'll have strawberry with strawberry syrup."

Ava, Adelaide, and Aria all looked at her.

"I know," Violet cut in. "It sounds too sweet but it's really good."

"Cool," said Ava with a shrug. "I'll try it sometime."

The man behind the counter called out their order to a woman by the ice-cream freezer. Then he announced the total price. That was why J.R. had said she wasn't thirsty. Since her mom was always with her, J.R. never carried money. Reluctantly, she opened the smallest pocket of her backpack and pretended to look inside. She would have to borrow from Violet and pay her back. "Sorry," J.R. started to apologize at the same time she saw something truly surprising: The pocket wasn't empty. Instead, there was a ten-dollar bill and a set of keys. She hadn't even thought about how she was going to get into her apartment. J.R. casually handed the money to Ava, who passed back her milkshake and some change. Then she took a long, deep sip, hoping to settle her racing heart. She definitely had not put that stuff in her bag.

"Delicious!" proclaimed Ava as she savored her first taste.

"So good!" Aria squealed. The sound was pretty jarring

and cut against the rumor that Aria's mom had been an opera singer before she moved from Argentina to New York.

"We should do this every day," Adelaide said, "now that we're Walkers!"

The other girls broke out in laughter. J.R. held up her milkshake to invite a group toast, then took a big sip. "I'm in," she said, before a brain freeze made her squint. At least for today, she was a Walker, and her milkshake was truly delicious.

"Hold that thought." Violet pulled out her phone and waited for J.R. to regain her composure before she took a picture. "#Mathildasmilkshakes #bffs," she said as she posted the photo. It hadn't actually occurred to J.R. that Violet would be on Instagram, too, now that she had a phone.

"Did you tag us?" Aria asked.

"Of course!" Violet looked apologetically at J.R. as soon as Aria turned away.

"Looks like you'll get rained out from soccer," Aria said to Adelaide as the girls stepped outside. Adelaide played for a different club and had scored on J.R. during their final game of the spring season. It was one of the moments when J.R. wished she played offense instead of defense. As they all looked up at the sky, Aria reached out and brushed at her friend's shoulder.

"What?" Adelaide asked.

"You're shedding red hair all over the place!" Aria held up a clump that she'd pulled off Adelaide's shirt.

"Strawberry blond," Adelaide corrected.

If Adelaide wanted to call it strawberry blond that was fair, but J.R. didn't like her tone. Aria had only been trying to help.

At the sound of distant thunder, all five girls ducked their heads, then started to walk north. Fast. When they reached the next corner, Violet broke off toward the conservatory where her orchestra had rehearsal. It didn't look easy with her cello on her back, her backpack on her front, and now a drink in her hand. She acknowledged the less-than-ideal situation with a self-deprecating grin.

J.R. thought she caught Adelaide giving Aria a look. She was tempted to leave with Violet, but it would have been weird since J.R. lived in the direction the rest of the girls were going.

"I'm excited for Saturday night!" Ava shouted as Violet crossed the street.

"Me too!" Violet called back. This time, there was no question that Adelaide sneered. J.R. tried hard, but she couldn't stop herself from wondering what they were doing on Saturday. Or really, it was more like worry than wonder.

One block later, Ava, Adelaide, and Aria headed west while J.R. went east, saying the quickest goodbye she could. As she walked and sipped her shake, her excitement returned and she had to try hard to act like everything was normal. J.R. nodded hello to the mailman collecting letters from a box and to the dog walker who had a monopoly on the neighborhood. She stopped to admire the mums outside her mom's favorite florist. When she reached her corner, J.R. even slowed down to look through the window into June's Books.

The store was small and square with shelves around the outside and potted plants in the corners. There was a table in the middle where customers could sit and leaf through books. It was named after Mr. Richardson's wife, a poet who J.R.'s parents told her had died when she was young. Her picture hung behind the old-fashioned cash register at the back of the store. Like a lot of people in the neighborhood, the Silvers kept an account at the store, billed monthly and recorded on index cards kept behind the counter. J.R. and Violet had both attended story hour at June's every Saturday when they were little, although it was hard to say which they liked more, the stories or the sliding ladder that moved across the shelves. Most places would never let kids play on the rungs, but Mr. Richardson said it was fine as long as parents supervised.

On Sunday mornings, before the store opened, June's hosted a small group of adults who were learning to read. Nic had a community service requirement in high school, and J.R. and Violet had already made a secret plan to volunteer on Sundays if Mr. Richardson would let them, although they would probably have to talk to him first. For all the time the girls had spent in June's, neither had spoken to Mr. Richardson all that much. He was quiet and usually let Maria, the manager, take the lead with customers, including the story hour kids. So while he was familiar company, J.R. would hardly call her neighbor a friend.

Mr. Richardson was definitely an exceptional host, however, and one of the best things about June's was the annual

holiday party in December. It seemed like everyone in the neighborhood stopped by to get gifts. There were cookies and mulled cider that made the whole room smell incredible. J.R.'s and Violet's families always met there to buy each other semi-secret books and then went back to Violet's apartment afterward for dinner. This year's party promised to be particularly festive because it was also the store's twenty-fifth birthday.

The only bad thing about June's was George, the black cat who liked to sun himself in the front windows. He triggered J.R.'s allergies and was particularly unfriendly, regularly hissing at customers.

As J.R. studied the window display, which was full of back-to-school books, Mr. Richardson waved from inside. He had brown skin and close-cut gray hair. He was a little older than her parents, but not by much. J.R. was tempted to go in and put the spilled-coffee incident behind her. But it had been a while since she left school, and it felt like she should hurry up and get home. She waved back and kept going. A few seconds later, the bells above the door jingled.

"Everything all right?"

J.R. froze. How had she blown it? How had she gotten all the way home without anyone asking why she was out alone, only to have Mr. Richardson stop her?

"Everything's fine," J.R. turned around and answered as confidently as she could. "Just heading home."

"The plan was for you to check in here first, though, right?" J.R. must have blanched. Mr. Richardson chuckled and held up his arms in mock surrender. "Don't worry. I'm not babysitting. Your parents just wanted to be sure you made it back safely, remember?"

J.R. definitely did not remember, and she did not want a babysitter, no matter what Mr. Richardson called it. "I really wouldn't want to bother you," she said, hoping to make the encounter end. "I can see you're busy." J.R. motioned to a woman with a stroller who was trying to open the door with one hand. She was talking on a phone lodged between her cheek and her shoulder, ignoring the NO CELL PHONES, PLEASE sign right in front of her.

"No bother at all. Tomorrow, just pop in and let me know you made it, okay?"

J.R. was truly taken aback by her parents' half-baked plan that they had somehow failed to mention to her. It wasn't Mr. Richardson's fault, though, and there was no use debating her neighbor. She would sort it out when her mom and dad got home. "No problem, Mr. Richardson," she said. "I won't forget."

"Sounds good," he replied, holding the door for the woman with the stroller. "No need to be so formal, though. Alex would be fine."

J.R. watched as he followed his customer into the store and said something quietly, presumably a reminder about the phone policy. She searched her memory for any instructions from her parents about checking in with Mr. Richardson, or Alex as he wanted to be called. Absolutely nothing came to mind.

Chapter 5

HALF A BLOCK AND ONE narrowly avoided pile of dog poop later, J.R. reached her building. The Silvers' brownstone was four stories tall, and they rented an apartment on the second floor. Mr. Richardson lived off the lobby, and the Li family had a duplex on three and four.

"Mom?" she called out when she made it upstairs and through their front door.

No one answered.

J.R. checked the living room, the kitchen, and her parents' bedroom, which doubled as her mom's office, but her mom wasn't home. Then she checked the kitchen one more time for good measure.

Climbing onto the windowsill behind the living room sofa, J.R. looked out at the street, where it had started to drizzle. The doorman in front of the building across the way stared forlornly at the sky. A grocery delivery team sprinted down the block with a trolley full of boxes, and a little boy stuck out his tongue to catch a few drops while he walked with his mom.

Caroline Silver was nowhere in sight.

J.R.'s nerves flared slightly. As she got down from the window, a clap of thunder confirmed that soccer practice was canceled. J.R. flipped the dead bolt on the front door, headed for her room, and hunted around in her hamper until she found her Nic sweatshirt. After a quick sniff, she decided it could handle one more wear. J.R. grabbed her ball from the corner and bounced it off her feet as she tried to work out what was going on. Her parents had definitely rejected this walking-home-alone scenario just the night before. So why hadn't her mom shown up for pickup? It would have been alarming, except that no one else at Nic had expected her mother to come, at least not Ms. Kline or Violet.

Lost in her thoughts, J.R. accidentally sent the soccer ball flying into her lampshade. Luckily, nothing broke, but it seemed like a sign she should stop. J.R. retrieved her personal journal from her pajama drawer, planted herself on her bed, and recorded a few observations about the day.

~ Everything normal until dismissal
~ Ms. Kline: Thought I was a Walker
~ Violet: Same
~ Mom: Where is she?
~ Alex Richardson—(not my) babysitter

Then she added one last note.

~ *Violet and Ava: What are they doing on Saturday?*

After sitting with the last line for a minute, J.R. realized she could hear the trickling of Mr. Richardson's frog fountain. His apartment was the only one allowed to use the small garden at the back, and he liked to putter around outside after work. Sometimes J.R. got curious. She wouldn't call it spying, but she occasionally found herself peering over the fire escape that ran between her window and her parents' bedroom to see what he was doing. The answer was usually watering the plants or reading a book. Even when no one was out there, the sound of the water arcing out of the frog's mouth and into the tiny pond by the back fence was soothing. J.R. was always sad when Mr. Richardson shut it off as the cold weather came in the fall.

One hour and a major downpour later, a key clicked in the Silvers' door. As J.R. popped out of her room, more noises echoed from the hallway before her mom, soaking wet, came in carrying groceries and asking why the door had been double-locked. J.R. was loath to confess to a case of home-alone nerves. "Sorry," she said. "I must have flipped the lock without thinking."

Her mom's expression said she wished her daughter would think.

J.R. took the bag of food and headed for the kitchen.

"How was school?" her mom called out as she put away her jacket and shoes in the coat closet.

"Good. How was work? Did you have a meeting this afternoon?" J.R. put two yogurts and a carton of eggs in the fridge before catching a whiff of overripe cheese.

"Nope, no meeting." Her mom came to the kitchen and scanned the food options before she excused herself to change her clothes, taking a couple of mini carrots with her.

That night at dinner, J.R. waited for her parents to say something about the afternoon, but neither of them did. Instead, her dad kept talking about a meeting that had gone badly. His avoidance of the most important topic of the day felt particularly frustrating since he kept using terms like "*that one*" and "you know who," which clearly meant something to J.R.'s mom but were meaningless to her. The problem was, J.R. couldn't tackle the subject of Mr. Richardson without raising the fact that she had walked home alone. What if there really had been some misunderstanding and her parents took everything back? When J.R. and her father finally loaded the dishwasher after dessert, her curiosity got the better of her.

"Big day, huh?" Inside her slippers, J.R. crossed her toes for good luck.

Her dad looked at his daughter as he passed her a soapy plate. "Sorry about all that work talk. How was the first day?"

"School started yesterday!" J.R. opened her eyes wide to show her incredulity. Then she took the plate and stuck it in the rack.

"That's what I thought. Remind me, why was today special?"

J.R.'s father was prone to playing little jokes, and she

started to wonder if he had graduated to big ones. Maybe her parents had planned to let her be a Walker all along but decided to make her sweat it first.

"It was special since you and Mom changed your minds without telling me?"

"Changed our minds about what?"

J.R. didn't have patience for teasing now that she realized the whole thing had been a ruse. "Changed your minds," she said while making air quotes, "about letting me be a Walker. I mean, I thought you two were totally against it. You definitely had me convinced."

Now her dad looked worried. "Is something wrong, sweetheart? Is it going to be too much, even if you check in at June's?"

"No!" J.R. spoke so fast she spat a little. "It's totally fine, and I don't need to check in with anyone."

Her dad's face went from worried to annoyed. "I thought we were all in agreement on this. It's easier for your mother if she doesn't have to do pickup, and we know how much you want to walk home with your friends. We're very proud of you for being responsible enough to do that, but I don't want to revisit checking in with Alex. I really don't think that's too much to ask, and it's nice of him to make himself available."

The intensity of her dad's reaction took J.R. by surprise. Being a Walker clearly was not one of his jokes. He was actually convinced they had discussed the whole plan already.

J.R. was equally certain that no such conversation had

occurred. She also knew when not to push her luck. "Okay, Dad. We'll do it your way. For now," she added, trying to defuse the situation even though she herself felt utterly confused. Luckily, her dad smiled back.

J.R. remained a Walker for the rest of the week, although she kept waiting for someone or something to break the spell. But every morning when she left for school and said, "See you tonight," neither of her parents flinched. When she joined the Walker line at dismissal, no one looked twice, either. And when she stopped dutifully at June's each afternoon, Alex simply asked if everything was all right and she told him that it was. The entire exchange took about ten seconds.

After a few days, her new life almost felt normal, and J.R. managed to forget about Violet's mysterious weekend plans until Friday afternoon, when Violet finally mentioned that she was going to Ava's beach house. J.R. wondered if her friend might not have said anything at all if J.R. hadn't been standing right there when Ava told Violet to be ready to go at eight o'clock. J.R. wanted to ask Violet more about their plans, but she didn't want to sound like she was fishing for an invitation, which she wasn't, or like she was feeling left out, which she was. "Don't you have orchestra rehearsal?" she asked instead, even though it wasn't her job to manage Violet's schedule.

"My mom said I could skip," Violet announced, "just this once." They both knew Violet never skipped orchestra.

Chapter 6

WHEN J.R. AND VIOLET WALKED into class on Monday morning, J.R. inquired about the weekend as casually as she could. She nodded along as Violet talked about the view from Ava's house, the awesome heated pool, and how lucky Ava was to have parents who let them make s'mores over a firepit and didn't care if they stayed up until the sun rose on Sunday. Violet said it was so fun that she didn't even feel tired.

The itinerary was impossible to compete with, and the timing made Violet's recounting worse. Over breakfast that morning, J.R.'s mom had offered to walk her and Violet through a new tapestry exhibit being installed at the Met. The idea had sounded fun at the time, but maybe not in comparison to what Ava could offer. Summoning her courage and reminding herself that Violet loved the museum as much as she did, J.R. asked if Violet wanted to go.

"That sounds cool," Violet started. "But I told Ava she could come over this afternoon, and now Aria wants to come, too. I doubt your mom was expecting four of us, so you should go without me."

"O-K," J.R. said slowly. It was too much work to hide her disappointment.

"Or you could come over, too, if you want?"

The invitation sounded sincere, but J.R. didn't feel like accepting. Instead, she mustered an excuse about not crowding into Violet's room that earned her a funny look. J.R. couldn't tell if her friend didn't believe her, or if Violet was insulted. Her bedroom actually was pretty small, and that probably hadn't been the best excuse to offer after Violet just finished talking about Ava's palace. Before J.R. could think of a way to clear things up, Violet shut the conversation down. "Next time?" she asked.

"Next time," J.R. confirmed. She turned away quickly as a lump grew in her throat.

On the verge of tears, J.R. was relieved to hear Ms. Kline clap three times, even though it was a technique that seemed more suited to a room full of preschoolers than sixth graders. The teacher asked the class to sit down, and then she passed back their *Gothamite* assignments. Now J.R.'s worries shifted. She definitely hoped her first story had made a good impression.

"Please be sure to read my comments," Ms. Kline instructed as she circled the room. "I've provided each of you with specific feedback, and I'll be looking for progress over the course of the semester. If you follow my advice, your writing will become more effective." Ms. Kline spoke in her usual slightly stilted manner, emphasizing the word "effective." Most people probably wouldn't have noticed, but J.R. found herself hanging on the teacher's every word. "I'm also giving each of you a folder in which to collect your *Gothamite* assignments. You're welcome to look back on them as you wish. In fact, I encourage you to do so."

"Not gonna happen," Curtis said, pretending to cough.

"What was that?" Ms. Kline asked with a fake-innocent look, like she had misheard him but she hadn't.

"Nothing," Curtis said quickly.

Their teacher didn't wait for further apology. "You'll see that I've pasted a *Gothamite* cover on the outside of your folders to make it easy for everyone to tell them apart. I hope you'll enjoy my selections."

Curtis held up his folder, scrunching his face in displeasure. The cover now decorating the front showed a bunch of people napping after a picnic, and the whole picture was bathed in yellow light.

"Silence is golden," Margaret muttered.

J.R. laughed in spite of herself. It was the first funny thing she had heard Margaret say.

Ms. Kline made her way around the room passing out folders with their stories inside. When Violet got hers, she flashed the picture in J.R.'s direction. It was the East Coast of North America with a parade of sea creatures heading north. Lobsters crawled toward Canada, and humpback whales followed.

Below them, a group of sea turtles swam off Delaware and manatees floated toward South Carolina. The animals were clearly all looking for colder water. J.R. made a sad face. It was a good picture for Violet, though, who joined Nic's Endangered Species Club each year.

"Here we are," Ms. Kline said when she finally handed J.R. her composition and the folder to keep it in. She gave a short, approving nod.

After Ms. Kline walked away, J.R. flipped to the comments, which were disappointingly short.

J.R.:

I can tell you know that words are powerful.
If you choose the right ones, your stories
will come alive. It's not easy, but I sense
you'll make smart choices. Tess felt like
a full and relatable character. Good work
getting inside her head.

J.R. reread the paragraph. It was hardly the detailed feedback she had been hoping for, but at least it was positive and Ms. Kline seemed to think she had succeeded in making Tess seem real.

The picture on the folder didn't make sense at all, though. Ms. Kline had chosen a cover from 1972 with a dance studio ringed by ballerinas in glistening swan costumes. Some were

55

whispering, others were watching. A stern man in black with floppy gray hair and long sideburns stood in the corner. He crossed his arms in front of his chest. The only person who looked like she was enjoying herself was a ballerina doing a giant leap in the middle of the room with her legs improbably parallel to the floor.

Ballet wasn't really J.R.'s thing. When her mom took her to see *Swan Lake*, the dark theater and wordless hours made her fall asleep. She felt pretty disappointed—why had Ms. Kline made that selection for her?

As J.R. started to read the comments on her story one more time, she noticed Violet passing Ava a note under their desks. J.R. got so engrossed in what they were doing that she didn't see Ms. Kline set out a new collection of *Gothamite* covers. The spell was broken when her teacher called out, "Violet and Ava!" The girls' heads shot up and their eyes went wide. "There will be no passing notes in this class. I will not ask to see what you wrote, but I will ask you to stop right now."

"We weren't really passing notes," Ava said. "I promise." Her voice quivered.

"We were playing hangman," Violet jumped in. "Ava chose 'onomatopoeia,' and I just got it right."

"Boom," Tommy said quietly. He was definitely the only boy in the class who could make an onomatopoeia joke.

"Well then, we won't get too hung up on that," Ms. Kline conceded.

"Pun intended?" Tommy asked under his breath.

"Not sure," J.R. whispered back. "She didn't crack a smile."

"Not her style."

J.R. accidentally snorted at the rhyme.

Margaret gave her a look.

"Please, everyone pay attention now," Ms. Kline said warily. "Here is a new set of *Gothamite* covers, and your assignment is to draft another first-person story. What I'd like you to focus on this time is voice. Is your narrator mature or immature? Long-winded or succinct? Silly or droll? What's distinctive about their style and speech?"

"What does droll mean?" Aria asked.

"I would define it as dryly amusing, perhaps in a slightly odd way." Tommy caught J.R.'s eye, and she bit her tongue to stop herself from laughing. "Who here chose *Born a Crime* for their memoir? Carlos?" Carlos looked up from doodling in his notebook, as usual. He was really good at drawing, so J.R. was kind of surprised he hadn't chosen the graphic memoir. "How would you describe Trevor Noah's voice in his book?"

"Um, funny?" Carlos answered.

"I agree," Ms. Kline said. "Is everything he writes about funny?" she asked.

"No," Carlos answered. "A lot of it's pretty terrible."

"That's right. And terribly unfair. But he alternates between funny and serious and loving, especially when he talks about his mom, to get his points across. I think it's really wonderful how he does it. So for your stories, I'd like you to

57

come up with your own unique way for your character to express themself, a unique way to see the world. Then combine that with enough plot to move things along and details to make the story come alive. Your goal is to break down the wall between the page and real life."

"What's that mean?" Tommy wrinkled his nose and forehead, clearly perplexed.

"Dunno," J.R. mouthed, mirroring his furrowed brow. Before she could figure it out, Ms. Kline told the class to make their picks.

J.R. rushed up from her seat, determined not to be stuck with the leftovers again. She pushed past Margaret and Tommy. Then, without knowing why, she pushed past four more kids, straight to the farthest cover she could find, propped in the window at the back of the classroom. It was a picture of a girl lying in bed beside a sunny window. There was a leafy green tree outside and a bluebird on the sill. The girl's face bore a mischievous expression, and she was pulling an iPad out from under her striped comforter with one hand while holding a thermometer up to the lamp beside her bed with the other. A calendar on her bedside table—the "word of the day" type—bore the word "thespian." J.R. chuckled. It was definitely the cover she wanted.

After everyone was set for the assignment, it was time for Play Street, which J.R. could already tell was a real misnomer. Up through fifth grade, each class went to recess as a homeroom

on the roof, which was pretty fun
even if the monkey bars got old.
In sixth grade, though, the whole
grade went outside and Nic Security closed the block to traffic. It
wasn't so bad for the boys, who
threw foam footballs or kicked
a soccer ball back and forth.
But the girls mostly gathered
around in groups to talk. Violet

beckoned J.R. over, but she didn't want to debate whether
Curtis was funny or whether Matt Ghent looked better with
his hair short or shaggy, both of which had already become
regular topics of discussion. Besides, the answers were obvious. Curtis was kind of funny but too mean. And Matt looked
cute with both haircuts, but that was about all J.R. knew
about him because he rarely talked after arriving at Nic last
year and sliding into the role of Curtis's silent sidekick. When
Play Street was almost over, J.R. needed a tissue for her still-
runny nose and asked for permission to head inside early. She
went to the bathroom and unwound some toilet paper. Someone sniffled in the stall beside her. Then the main door opened
and a bigger sniffle followed.

"Are you all right in there?" J.R. recognized the voice
immediately. It was Violet, but no one answered. "Hey, are
you okay?" Violet asked again.

"I'm okay," the other girl said. J.R.'s own stall door had closed behind her, and neither of the other two girls realized she was there.

"Do you need help?" The metal door beside J.R. squeaked as it opened. "Oh," said Violet. "What happened?"

"I forgot where the bathroom was." The girl sounded young, and Nic's layout could be confusing.

"It's no big deal," Violet assured her. "What's your name?" The girl hesitated. "I'm not going to tell; I just want to find your locker. You have extra clothes in there, right?"

Little Elizabeth Rhodes shared her name and described the picture of a sun she had drawn for the front of her locker so Violet could easily find it. Violet promised to be right back before she sent Elizabeth to wait in her stall and went to retrieve the dry outfit. J.R. snuck out as soon as she could. She replayed the conversation in her head for the rest of the afternoon. It reminded her that Violet had a big heart, and that Violet was a friend worth fighting for.

Chapter 7

WHEN SCHOOL ENDED, J.R. COULDN'T stomach the idea of watching Aria and Ava set off for Violet's apartment. Rather than leave with the group, she made up an excuse about needing a book from the library, then lingered by her locker. She hung around so long, in fact, that when she finally opened the stairway door to leave she ran straight into Ms. Kline, who was coming back from dismissing the Greeters.

"Enjoy tonight's assignment," Ms. Kline said as she waved J.R. onto the landing. "I hope you do something nice with it." Her voice was cheery, but her eyes bored into her student in a way that didn't seem friendly at all.

J.R. promised to do so and set off toward the lobby. She didn't hear the fire door close behind her until she reached the fourth floor. Apparently, Ms. Kline had lingered as well. "Click," J.R. muttered. "Now there's an onomatopoeia for you."

J.R. stopped at June's on the way home, as she was now accus-
tomed to doing. If Alex was with a customer, he would look
up when the bells jingled. Then J.R. would mouth hello and
continue on her way to do homework or get ready for soccer.
Alex's store manager, Maria, was often around, too, and if
Alex was in the back, J.R. would check in with her instead.
Maria had curly brown hair with blond tips, and she always
wore a signature cherry-colored lipstick. Around the bookstore, there were little white cards on the shelves with short
recommendations for books they liked. J.R. could tell that
Maria had written the review if there were red lips stamped
in the corner. Alex's cards had green reading glasses like the
ones he kept by the cash register.

J.R. still didn't understand exactly how she had become a
Walker, or how her parents had made their plan with Alex,
so it seemed safer to keep her daily check-ins short. With Violet hosting Aria and Ava, though, she didn't feel like going
home right away and being alone. So when J.R. got to the
store that afternoon, she scanned the room for a place to drop
her backpack. Maria was refilling a shelf of early readers, and
Alex was picking yellow leaves off a flowerless geranium in
the window.

"You can slide it under there." Alex pointed to the wooden
benches on either side of the door. Behind the one on the
right, there was a special shelf that Alex reserved for books

by writers who had just published their first novel. Behind the other bench, Maria curated a section of books in Spanish, everything from picture books to poetry. J.R. stashed her bag on the Spanish side, then made her way to the middle grade section along the opposite wall. She started by looking through the Ss since she liked to imagine seeing "J.R. Silver" there one day.

"Looking for something special?"

"Not really." J.R. didn't want to tell Alex that she was actually looking for a story that would take her mind off things. Then, surprising herself, she asked if he had any recommendations, although still keeping the details of what she wanted to read to herself.

"Let's see." The bookseller came over and ran his finger across a few titles until he found what he was looking for. "Read this one yet?"

J.R. took the book and skimmed the back. It was about identical twin sisters who were inseparable until their parents got divorced and each twin took one parent's side. "Not sure about that," she said. She didn't love his next two suggestions, either, neither of which promised to offer a sufficient escape. Rather than keep turning him down, she thanked Alex for the ideas and said she'd try another time. Then she retrieved her backpack and headed home.

Outside in the sun, though, J.R. still wasn't ready to retreat to her room. She considered her options and headed west with a destination in mind. It was only a small detour, she told herself, and she would be quick.

Just before reaching Central Park, J.R. veered through a wrought iron fence and onto the lawn behind the Cooper Hewitt Museum, which had the most amazing towers of vines covering its brick facade. They were leafy, twisted, and huge, and Jack's beanstalk definitely would have been jealous. Better even than the vines—although maybe only because the former weren't actually available for climbing—were the Cooper Hewitt's chairs, a handful of bright red, heavy plastic sculptures that looked like the top of a thumbtack with an

indentation on top to sit in. They touched the ground on a point and could spin around 360 degrees before coming to rest at a slight angle. J.R. sat in a chair and twirled around until she felt ill. Then she put her feet down to make the spinning stop.

J.R. opened up her backpack and pulled out her newest *Gothamite* cover. A story idea was on the tip of her tongue, but she couldn't quite get it out. With the picture in her lap, J.R. tipped the chair back carefully so that her head was lower than her knees and her legs dangled over the side. She practiced straightening them, which required trusting the chair not to fall, and then bent them again to be more comfortable. Resting the cover on her stomach, she closed her eyes and listened to a bus barrel down Fifth Avenue, and to two girls squeal as they ran around the lawn. A Ping-Pong ball clicked back and forth on the table nearby.

"I thought that was you!"

J.R. opened her eyes to see Tommy standing over her. He had changed into his soccer uniform and appeared to be headed for practice. "Oh, hey," she said, instantly self-conscious about being upside down. J.R. tipped the chair forward until her feet hit the ground with a graceless thud.

"Don't get up on my account." Tommy grabbed a chair and rolled it over. "What are you reading?"

"Nothing," J.R. answered. "I was just thinking about our creative writing assignment."

Tommy held out his hand, and J.R. took advantage of the stiff lamination to toss her cover to him like it was a Frisbee. "Funny how much she looks like Ava, right?"

"Huh?"

"I mean, the blond hair and bangs." Tommy pointed to the girl in the picture. "And she's got those blue pajamas that are the same color as the shirt Ava was wearing today. Plus, there's the dimple."

Tommy rotated the picture so J.R. could get a better look, but she was distracted by the fact of his observations. How come he remembered exactly what Ava had worn that day? She wondered if he would have remembered what *she* was wearing. Tommy was right, though, about the similarities, including the dimple. It highlighted the girl's plotting grin as she warmed a thermometer against her lamp. Ava had a dimple, too, and J.R. sometimes wondered if she practiced smiling to show it off.

"Good call," J.R. said, taking in the picture. "Thanks!"

"For what?" Across the lawn, Tommy's manny looked up from his phone long enough to call out a warning that they were going to be late for soccer. "Gotta go, but you're welcome!"

J.R. reached to take the cover back, now eager for Tommy to leave. Although initially disconcerting, his observations had inspired her. J.R. imagined Ava pretending to be sick, or maybe Ava really would get sick with something mild, but bad enough to keep her home. That could be the premise of J.R.'s story. After all, Ms. Kline had said not to interpret the covers too literally, and the girl in the cover was clearly faking it. J.R. relished the thought of a few days off from Violet's new friend. She shoved the cover back in her bag and walked quickly home, where she went straight to her room, retrieved her headband and slippers, and started to write. Feeling inspired and giddy, she decided to use a punchy voice as the distinctive tone Ms. Kline had asked for. She started with a title that she thought was particularly clever.

WISH COME TRUE

Ouch! Double ouch! Triple ouch!
That's what I thought in the middle of the night when I woke up. My ear hurt. My throat hurt. And my head hurt, too. It was a trifecta!

> I called for my mom, but only a croak came out. This wasn't what I had in mind when I went to bed wishing I'd wake up sick. I just wanted a little something—a chill, maybe—so I could take a day off. Admittedly, it wasn't a coincidence that it was a day with a spelling quiz.

J.R. went back and added parentheses around the last sentence, using the punctuation to create what her counselor at summer camp had described as a written wink.

> When my sister poked her head in and said, "Holy zombie," I knew things were bad. I must have really looked awful, judging by how fast she fled my germs.
> Staying home was one thing, but actually being sick was another. I just wanted one day when I could cuddle with Rocky, watch TV, and maybe eat chicken soup, preferably in bed.

J.R. heard the story start unfolding in Ava's voice.

> I'm sweating and shivering, and it hurts to swallow. I reach for the gold four-leaf clover that usually hangs from a chain around my neck before I remember that I had taken it off.

Figures!

Mom says we're going to see Dr. Moss at noon, which is the worst news of all. I'm too old to sit in that waiting room with Big Bird posters and chewed-up books.

J.R. thought about Ms. Kline's instruction to use details to make the story feel real—to break down the wall between the page and real life, whatever that meant. She decided to get pretty specific.

What if he gives me bad news and says I can't go back to school this week? We've got the Statue of Liberty trip tomorrow, and Alexis's birthday on Friday. I will be SO BUMMED to miss those.

Plus, I promised Catie I'd be her bus partner since I was Mia's partner for the Tenement Museum trip last month. Catie won't be happy if I don't show up.

This home-sick thing is a disaster. I need to brush this knot out of my hair and then close my eyes for a minute. I'm really, really tired. All this worrying is taking a lot out of me, too. But not as much out of me as that spelling quiz would have!

J.R. added a smiley face at the end, which felt like something Ava would do. "Sleep well," she said as she put down her pen and closed her notebook. It would be kind of funny, in a not funny way, if Ava got sick like J.R. got to be a Walker. Impossible, of course, but still interesting to think about.

Chapter 8

"LET'S GET STARTED," MS. KLINE said the next morning after everyone settled into their seats.

"I think we're still waiting for Ava," Adelaide chimed in.

"Unfortunately, Ava is home sick."

J.R. felt her jaw drop, pulling the rest of her head down with it.

"You okay?" Tommy asked.

J.R. closed her mouth, then looked over at Violet. The fingers on her left hand were frozen at odd angles under her desk, since she had been practicing her cello without realizing it. Apparently, the news surprised Violet, too. When Tommy repeated his question, J.R. nodded.

"Poor girl," Ms. Kline continued. "I understand her symptoms came on suddenly. If anyone else feels sick, please be sure to let your parents know. Strep throat is very contagious, so I do hope it doesn't spread." Ms. Kline began circling the classroom to collect the previous night's work. J.R. sat completely still.

"You didn't do yours?" Tommy asked.

"Huh?" J.R. wished he would stop talking. She needed a second to think.

"Did you not do the homework?" Tommy held up his assignment, which had at least five pages of paper stapled together even though Ms. Kline said they only had to write two.

"No, I did it." In her mind, J.R.'s words came out like a slow-speaking demon. Reality definitely felt twisted. She pulled out her homework and skimmed through the pages. She had to fight the urge to plant her elbows on her desk and put her head in her hands, and instead try to snap out of this strange dream. Writing the story the night before, J.R. had felt like a toddler scribbling a picture to work through her frustration. She never really believed that the story would come true.

"May I have your work?" Ms. Kline held out her hand.

"It's just—" J.R. started. She was so bewildered that she didn't even notice the whole class looking at her.

"Yes?"

"It's just—" J.R. swallowed. Would Ms. Kline recognize the similarities between the girl in her story and J.R.'s actual classmate? Even if she did, what conclusion would she draw?

Ms. Kline cleared her throat, which had the effect of rubbing in the fact that Ms. Kline's throat was fine, unlike the girl's in J.R.'s story, and unlike Ava's, too. "If you don't mind passing me your assignment, I look forward to reading it."

J.R. glanced at her short story one more time. Unable to keep stalling, she handed it over, along with the magazine cover.

Ms. Kline finished collecting assignments, tapped the set of papers into a neat pile, and put them on her desk alongside the laminated magazines. "We don't have too much time this morning," she said. "But I thought we could still do a quick writing exercise." J.R. held her breath, hoping for another *Gothamite* project. "I'm going to give each of you a new cover—my choice this time—and I want you to write a very short scene. Be creative," she instructed, "and go with your instincts. If you start to second-guess yourself, don't. Think of this as a sprint, where your goal is simply to get words out on paper."

This is it, J.R. thought as she watched Ms. Kline walk through the room. If what appeared to be happening really was—if she could make things happen just by writing them— now was the time to find out.

"You seem anxious to get started," Ms. Kline said as she gave a cover to Tommy. Meanwhile, her eyes never left J.R.

"I'm just enjoying these assignments." J.R. smiled sweetly at her teacher. She realized she was drumming her fingers on her desk and laid her palm down flat to stop.

"Let me see." Ms. Kline turned to Margaret next. She thumbed through her stack, then handed over a picture of the main branch of the New York Public Library. Two stone lions, known as Patience and Fortitude, kept watch out front.

The leaves on the trees were orange, and the artist had drawn a navy-and-white scarf around Patience's neck, and a bright blue-and-orange one around Fortitude's.

Margaret looked puzzled.

"What's the date?" Tommy asked.

Margaret checked the picture. "October 30, 2000."

"Subway Series," Tommy and Carlos said in unison.

Next, Ms. Kline picked an image for Carlos. It was a picture of three men sitting on the subway. Each held open a newspaper so his face was obscured. J.R. could tell that the cover was old by the hats popping out over the papers and the formal shoes and dress pants sticking out from the bottom.

"Trade?" Carlos asked Margaret.

"Don't trade, just write," Ms. Kline instructed.

Finally, it was J.R.'s turn. Her teacher leafed through her pile several times, pausing to consider various options. J.R. wished she could see the images Ms. Kline was rejecting. She reminded herself to breathe.

After a third time through the stack, Ms. Kline selected a cover that had been published during the last Women's World Cup. J.R. let out an audible sigh of relief. It was drawn from the point of view of a spectator sitting directly behind a little girl who was watching the game on the edge of her seat. One goalie lay on the ground in front of the net, while a player from the opposing team ran gleefully toward her teammates with her arms up in the air.

J.R. looked over at Tommy, who was studying his selection,

a picture of Midtown Manhattan from the perspective of a migrating Canada goose.

"Bird's-eye view?" he suggested.

J.R. chuckled but was anxious to start writing. Advice she had once read from E. L. Konigsburg, the author of the *Mixed-Up Files*, popped into her head. Konigsburg said that when writing stories, she liked to take normal situations and ask *What if?* Something like "What if we ate ice cream for breakfast and toast for dessert?" or, presumably, "What if two children went to the Met and didn't leave?"

What if J.R. scored a game-winning goal? Taking on the persona of a rapid-fire TV announcer, she wrote as fast as she could as soon as Ms. Kline started the clock.

¡GOOOOOOL!

Greeden winds up for a long ball, but her teammates aren't giving her a lot of options.

Oh my, she decides to take it up the field herself.

And she gets to midfield, but Stevens and Manley are under pressure so she doesn't have a lot of options. Greeden's got to pass the ball somewhere, and Manley gets open. Beautiful move.

Looks like Greeden sees Manley, but something's up. Greeden keeps going. I think

she's going to take a shot. She's got a chance to
be the hero. She's going to shoot. She shoots.
She scores!!!!!

J.R. went back and underlined the first letter of the first word in each of the four paragraphs to make clear that they spelled out "GOAL."

Greeden was her mother's maiden name.

J.R.'s next game was on Sunday.

She played defense and had never scored in a game before, something she always wanted to do.

It was impossible to imagine having to wait a whole five days, but J.R. was sure the story was a test. If the magazine magic was real, her next match would be unforgettable in more ways than anyone else knew.

Chapter 9

J.R. WAS SO DISTRACTED BY the day's events that she forgot to stop by June's after school. Back home, she put on her writer's accessories and plopped down on the floor of her room, too agitated to do any homework. After staring at a blank page, she bounced back up with her journal, retrieved her soccer ball from the corner, and dribbled it through the apartment, stopping quickly at the fridge. As usual, there weren't a lot of good options, but J.R. managed to find a lonely stick of string cheese. Then she dribbled back to the living room, where she sat down on the couch, peeled off strands of mozzarella, and dangled them over her mouth as she thought. When she was done eating, J.R. jotted down a few similarities between her story and what happened that day.

The list didn't feel very satisfying. Granted, J.R. had made the sick girl a lot like Ava with her age, and puppy, and focus on friends. But writers often took inspiration from people they knew, like A. A. Milne, who modeled Christopher Robin on his own son when he wrote *Winnie-the-Pooh*. Using real life as inspiration was normal for an author. Altering real life through stories was *not*. Something very weird was happening.

Hit by a rush of curiosity, J.R. fished her mom's iPad out of the basket beside the couch. Then she typed "Kate Kline" into the search bar. None of the initial results were useful. Instead, she found a math professor in Manchester, England, the head of human resources for a manufacturing company in Michigan, and a Kate Kline who had been arrested in Boston for robbing an ice-cream store. The last article didn't include a photo, but she certainly hoped that wasn't her Kate Kline.

There was no sign of the woman J.R. was looking for, even when she added terms like "teacher" and "Northeast Kingdom" to her search.

J.R. ran her fingers lightly across the screen. Then she typed in "Eleanor Mendell," the woman who gave Ms. Kline the magazines. This time she found something.

> Wiscasset, Maine – Over three hundred people attended the funeral today for Eleanor Mendell, a longtime summer resident of Wiscasset. Mendell was a schoolteacher who taught in countless places, judging from conversations with many former students.
>
> "She really shaped my career even though I met her when I was only twelve," said Andrea Yellen, a

communications director from Washington, D.C., who was accompanied by Harry Collins, a cartoonist who said that Mendell was his teacher in Milwaukee.

"Eleanor Mendell was a force," said Alex Richardson, a bookseller who came up through New York City's public schools. "I even met my wife at a reunion for Eleanor's students. Eleanor was the one who convinced her to become a poet." Although he admitted that it was unusual to have a teacher-based reunion, Richardson said Mendell was simply that special.

"She helped me find my voice," said Darren Sweeney, a hostage negotiator for the Seattle Police Department who grew up in Mississippi, where Mendell taught his sixth-grade class.

"Eleanor was certainly the most influential teacher in my life," said Kate Kline, who became a teacher herself.

Several mourners were overheard speculating about whether Mendell had left a will and where her magazine collection would go in the wake of her passing. No attendees were available to comment on the latter.

J.R. considered the article, or maybe it was an obituary. She wasn't sure, since it was more about the funeral guests than about Ms. Mendell herself. Two names stuck out: the bookseller, Alex Richardson, and the teacher named Kate Kline. It wasn't a surprise to see Ms. Kline quoted, but having an Alex Richardson appear, with a poet wife, seemed like quite a coincidence.

Nothing in the article explained what seemed to be happening to J.R., although it did mention magazines. Nor did it reveal much about Ms. Kline—in fact, Ms. Kline said less about herself than anyone else who was interviewed. Still, J.R. had a hard time shaking the feeling that her teacher knew more than she was letting on, and now she suspected Alex did, too.

J.R. kept searching, but it soon became clear there would be no further clues on the internet. She needed to talk to someone, and the person she wanted to talk to first was Violet. In normal circumstances, J.R. would have told her best friend about the Walker story as soon as it happened. But normal circumstances didn't involve Ava. And how could she broach the subject now when her last writing effort seemed to have made Ava sick? Still, she needed her friend's advice, and Violet was good at keeping secrets—J.R. certainly didn't want to share her news widely. She picked up the phone and had just started to dial when she heard a knock from the hallway. J.R. wanted to ignore it, but a voice called her name. "I think she's here," she heard Alex say as she headed toward the foyer. "I'll call you back when I know more."

J.R. cringed. How could Alex have ratted her out to her

parents? "Sorry," she said as she opened the door, not waiting for Alex to talk. "I forgot to stop by, but I'm home, safe and sound. Was that my mom or my dad you were talking to?" Depending on the answer, she would come up with an appropriate plan to appease them.

"No, no. Just a friend." Alex glanced down at the phone in J.R.'s hand. "I'm the one who should apologize for interrupting," he said, although his expression was more curious than sorry. "Are you on with someone?"

"Nope. I'm about to be, though." J.R. raised her eyebrows as if to ask if he had any other questions. She knew it wasn't very polite, but she wanted Alex to go. "I need to make a quick call, and then I've got a ton of homework."

"Glad you made it back," Alex said slowly, glancing again at J.R.'s phone. "Maria and I were about to unpack a new shipment. Want to help us shelve the books? Then you'd get first pick." His question was odd. J.R. had just told him she was busy. She'd even invoked homework, since adults rarely argued with school obligations.

"I totally get it," Alex said when J.R. declined. "Homework comes first. I'll set aside a couple of books for you anyway. Mum's the word, okay?" Alex looked at J.R. hopefully, but kind of seriously, too.

"Sure," she answered, for lack of a better response. It was hard to tell exactly what Alex was talking about.

"Do I remember correctly that you're a *Mixed-Up Files* fan?" J.R. said she was, although she wished that Alex wouldn't keep the conversation going. "It's a great book." He bit his bottom lip gently, like he was pondering the novel. "Good ending, too, with how much Claudia and Mrs. Frankweiler have in common."

And that was it. Without saying more, Alex held up a hand to signal goodbye and headed for the stairs. J.R. closed the door and went straight to the living room, where she looked out the window until Alex appeared, like she somehow knew he would, on his phone and walking back toward June's. J.R. wondered who he was talking to—who he was reporting to, she suspected—since it wasn't her parents. With no way to know, she plopped down on the couch and placed her call. When the Fernandos' babysitter, Nina, answered, J.R. asked for Violet.

"She's not here, darling. Her mom took her to get flowers for a girl who has the flu."

J.R.'s heart sank. "You mean strep," she corrected without really meaning to.

"Strep throat, you're right. Is the girl in your class? I think they were going to leave the flowers with the doorman, so they should be back soon. No hitting!" Nina called out. The twins were fighting loudly in the background.

J.R. declined Nina's offer to leave a message and got off as quickly as she could. Remaining on the couch, she replayed her encounter with Alex in her head. It seemed curious that he arrived just when she was about to call Violet, and who had he been talking to? Then there was his comment about the *Mixed-Up Files* and what Claudia and Mrs. Frankweiler have in common. That part, at least, was easy: They both like having a secret.

J.R. wished she felt the same way. Instead, she was tired of keeping her secret. It would be a lot more fun, she thought, if she had someone to share it with.

Chapter 10

J.R. DIDN'T HAVE ANY LUCK talking to Violet for the rest of the week, either. Ava was still out sick, but J.R. could never find the right way to bring up the magazines when the girls were together, and the failed phone call somehow left her feeling like the conversation would be better to have in person. The closest J.R. got was when Ms. Kline paired them up to study Norse mythology, which was made more fun by the fact that Ms. Kline brought in cone-shaped Norwegian cookies stuffed with cream that she called krumkake. She learned how to bake them, she said, when she taught in Minnesota. After Violet and J.R. made it twice through the list of gods they had to memorize, and through two rounds of cookies, J.R. asked nonchalantly if Violet had noticed anything unusual about Ms. Kline.

Violet thought before answering. "There does seem to be something odd about her. It's like she's always watching and maybe doesn't approve of what she sees. But on the other hand, she's also kind of fun, or at least unusual."

J.R. should have known that Violet would sum up Ms. Kline perfectly. Although, of course, this time J.R. was actually looking for a little bit more. Before she could ask another question, Violet continued, "Ava says Ms. Kline reminds her of a modern-day Mary Poppins. She's got her hair in a bun and the black clothes she always wears. Then there's the fact that she kind of blew in with the wind from Vermont. Good one, right?" Violet didn't wait for J.R. to answer. "If only she used some magic to make us fly."

The Mary Poppins comparison was really good, and J.R. was a little miffed she hadn't thought of it herself. *Speaking of magic*, she wanted to say.

"Don't look now," Violet whispered, which of course made J.R. look. Ms. Kline was watching from the corner and cocked her head when she caught J.R.'s eye.

On second thought, maybe it wasn't a good time to tell Violet that their teacher might be more like Mary Poppins than she and Ava realized.

J.R. finally caught a break on Friday. Violet wanted to stop by June's to get a birthday present for Nina. The girls went to Mathilda's on the way, and this time they both ordered strawberry shakes with strawberry syrup.

"So what's he like?" Violet asked as they got close to the bookstore, sucking down the last of her drink. J.R. waited for the gurgling noise to end before she answered.

"Who?"

"Mr. Richardson."

"I don't really know," J.R. admitted. "I usually say hi and go home. We don't talk a lot, although he told me to call him Alex, not Mr. Richardson."

"Fair enough. I bet that was just your parents trying to get you to be extra polite since he's your neighbor." J.R. shrugged, but it was probably true. "My mom said his wife was a really great poet, but she died before she could become famous." J.R. wondered what it took to become a famous poet these days. She was curious what type of poetry June had written, and whether any of her books were on the shelves in the store. "Why do you think he's doing it?" Violet asked.

"Doing what?"

"Babysitting!" Violet had laughed so hard in empathetic frustration when J.R. told her about her after-school arrangements—or at least about most of them, excluding their mysterious origin story.

"It's not babysitting, remember? Just checking in," J.R. called after Violet, who had veered off toward a garbage can to throw out her empty drink. J.R. took one last sip and tossed hers in after.

"How well do your parents really know him? Shouldn't you just ask them what's up?"

"No!" J.R. said a little too forcefully. That was the last thing she wanted to do. Checking in with Alex was part of something bigger, and stranger, and as yet unexplained. J.R.

was pretty sure of it, and she couldn't risk rocking the boat. "I mean, he does know my parents, since they go to the store, too, and he's lived in our building longer than we have. I guess they figured it's no big deal for me to stop in so that someone knows I'm getting home."

"And since you still don't have a phone," Violet teased.

J.R. scowled. "Besides, it really isn't a big deal. Sometimes I just open the door and barely go inside." What she really wanted to say was that Violet should follow her lead and leave well enough alone. Instead, she decided to remain vigilant. Hopefully, Violet wouldn't try to help. That was bound to mess things up.

When the girls reached June's, Alex was alone and sorting through a pile of mail behind the counter. "How was school?" he called out. Then he paused to examine an envelope before putting it aside.

"Good," the girls both answered.

J.R. looked at her friend warily. Violet's talkativeness did not bode well.

"That's more enthusiasm than I usually get," Alex said. "Anything I can help you two with?"

Violet dropped her backpack next to J.R.'s usual spot beneath the bench. Then she began to look through the cookbooks. "I need something for my babysitter's birthday, but I have an idea already." It was hard to tell if Violet had emphasized the word "babysitter" or if J.R. was just being sensitive.

She didn't even mind when Violet started texting. At least that would keep any conversation with Alex to a minimum.

Curious to learn more about June Richardson, J.R. headed for the small section of poetry in the back. She skimmed the shelves, but there was nothing under the Rs, and J.R. realized she didn't actually know June's last name. She pulled out a few books that looked interesting, but when she flipped to the author photos at the back, all the poets were men.

"All set," Violet called out, cookbook in hand, as J.R. gave up.

"What did you find?" Violet turned her selection around to show Alex the apple pie on the cover.

"Are you just trying to get Nina to make you more desserts?" Violet's babysitter was famous for her snickerdoodles. J.R. actually preferred her brownies, which were more than simple chocolate squares. Nina called them turtles, and they had layers of caramel and chopped nuts inside.

Violet scowled. Then she looked concerned. "Um," she said, eyeing the EMPLOYEES ONLY sign above the back door. Alex had written the words in his distinctive cursive, so the message was more friendly than foreboding. "Would you mind if I used your bathroom? I really have to pee."

"TMI," J.R. said.

"Go right ahead." Alex was more forgiving. "I'll wrap that for you in the meantime."

Violet headed to the back as Maria emerged with a catalog

in hand. "They've got some great stuff in here." She pointed to a display of Mylar balloons shaped like numbers from zero to nine. Maria had already begun planning that year's holiday party, since it was also a special anniversary for the business. Alex didn't seem as excited.

J.R. found a new graphic novel and asked to put it on her parents' account as George jumped up on the counter. When she reached to pet his back, the cat swiped at her.

"Silver, right?" Maria flipped through the box of index cards, unfazed by George's acrobatic hostility. J.R. nodded and checked her hand for scratches. Maria added the title and price to the Silvers' account and handed the book back to J.R. "Let me know if it's good? I've been curious about that one." As Maria started to clear off the countertop, she held up a letter. "What's Riley, Riddle & Mott?"

Alex quickly grabbed the envelope. "Nothing," he said brusquely, which wasn't like him at all. "Nothing to worry about."

"Who was worrying?" Maria didn't look convinced, but Violet reemerged from the back before she could press her boss any further.

"Where did you get that *Gothamite* cover?" Violet asked Alex. "Is that you and your wife?" She pulled J.R. toward the back to see. A framed magazine cover hung inside a small office above a messy desk. It was a drawing of a man in a brown suit kissing a woman in a wedding dress. Instead of a veil, the bride wore a white ribbon tied behind her ears that hung down past her shoulders. She was carrying a quill pen and scroll in one hand, and they were standing outside the front of June's. J.R. walked into the office for a closer look. Something was a little off. The font where it said *Gothamite* didn't look quite right, and on the bottom corner someone had written, "Congratulations! My love, HC."

Alex joined them. "Actually, that was a wedding present, not a real magazine. It was kind of a joke."

"So awesome, right?" Violet turned to J.R.

"Who's HC?" J.R. asked slowly.

"Harry Collins. He's an old friend and a cartoonist. We met at a reunion, a party, really, for a teacher we both had back when we were your age. I actually met June that same night."

J.R.'s ears perked up, recalling Ms. Mendell's obituary.

"Cool!" said Violet. "I hope someone puts me on the cover of a magazine someday, maybe even a real one."

Violet kept talking, but J.R. stopped listening. These multiplying coincidences were increasingly suspicious. But with Violet there, it wasn't the right time for J.R. to probe.

The wait for soccer was excruciating, although at least it provided some distraction. Violet and Ava were going to a Wachusett reunion on Saturday, which they had talked about all week. If J.R. hadn't been so excited to test her storytelling powers, she would have spent the whole time jealous. Luckily, the feeling that something good was coming swelled inside her all weekend, and J.R. had to try impossibly hard not to do anything suspicious.

By the time her team warm-up started on Sunday, J.R. was ready to burst. When she stretched, she bent from the waist and got her palms flat on the ground more easily than usual. When they played knockout, J.R. kicked six balls out of the circle without losing her own. And in their one-on-one drill, she beat Miranda to the ball. No one ever beat Miranda, although J.R. appreciated that her teammate never gloated. Nor did she pout in the face of J.R.'s unanticipated achievement.

Finally, the game started. J.R. kept looking for her breakout moment, but nothing happened. She wanted to dribble up the field, fake left, go right, and score. Or to weave around a defender, pass the ball to Miranda, and at least get an assist. Instead, she had three pretty good defensive plays that would have been a really good showing on a normal day. But when she tried to dodge one of the other team's wingers, the girl took the ball away and scored. Nothing spectacular had happened by halftime, and J.R. only touched the ball a couple of times after they started up again. When the game was tied with two minutes left and her team had lost all momentum, J.R. was crushed. Even more disappointing than the impending tie and lack of personal scoring, she was starting to doubt her storytelling magic.

"Go, Red Devils!" a boy cheered from the end of the field. J.R. looked over and saw Tommy, suited up in his navy blue

uniform. His love of sports wasn't a reflection of great athleti-
cism, and J.R. wasn't surprised to see he was a sub.

"Go, Nighthawks!" she shouted as Tommy's coach waved
him back toward the Nighthawks' sideline. J.R. refocused on
her game after the ball went out-of-bounds. She jogged over
to take the throw-in.

"Hustle, J.R.," Coach Mike shouted. J.R. cringed and hustled.

With two hands over her head, she threw the ball to Clara
P., who dribbled up the sideline. J.R. ran to the middle behind
Clara S., who received a pass and dumped the ball immediately on Miranda. Clara S. played so timidly that J.R. never
understood why she played soccer at all. But if there was anyone who could break the tie it was Miranda, so at least she
had given the ball to the right person. J.R. trailed to Miranda's
right as she dribbled toward the goal, weaving around two
defenders easily.

And then the ball was free. Somehow Miranda had missed
the girl coming from her left. J.R. didn't even need to adjust
her path, because the loose ball came straight to her. She
trapped it, dribbled a few more steps downfield, kicked hard,
and watched. The ball launched up and over the goalie's outstretched arms, and plowed deep into the net.

J.R. threw both arms in the air as her teammates converged
into a jumping hug. On the sidelines, Coach Mike threw his
hands into the air in celebration, J.R.'s mom shouted something unintelligible, and her dad accepted a congratulatory
handshake from Clara P.'s father.

Tommy cheered from the corner of his field, where he was purportedly playing defense.

"Watch out!" J.R. called just in time for Tommy to see the ball coming straight at him.

"Focus, Tommy!" his coach shouted.

J.R. peeked out of the scrum and caught sight of the other team's goalie, who looked crushed. J.R. looked away.

"That was so awesome!" Miranda gave J.R. a giant hug after the rest of the team headed back to their positions.

"Thanks! It felt incredible!" J.R. gushed. The words were true, but she couldn't tell Miranda precisely what she was thinking: The goal felt good—but the magic was real, and that felt amazing.

Chapter 11

With everyone still giddy for both obvious and less-than-obvious reasons, J.R.'s mom ordered pizza and let J.R. and her dad eat on the couch after the game. In the Silver family, such behavior was unheard-of.

"Could be another trip to the Super Bowl," her dad said, watching the Giants convert on fourth and one. The team looked good, but J.R. wasn't as optimistic. Her dad had the Sunday crossword puzzle open on his lap, so she asked for a clue. He scanned the list until he found one she could solve.

"Swedish winter drink."

"Glogg!" J.R. answered immediately. Last year, they had engaged in lengthy experiments with hot wine, lemon, and spices while trying to replicate a mug of glogg that her father had consumed on a work trip to Stockholm.

J.R.'s dad looked back through the list. "Chair in the sky."

"Cassiopeia," J.R. answered. She had known the answer in class earlier that week, too, when Ms. Kline quizzed them on constellations. She made a mental note to tell Tommy about the clue.

J.R.'s dad gave a thumbs-up but then got distracted by a Giants touchdown. Eventually he put down the puzzle.

J.R. was too excited for football to hold her attention. She kept thinking about what story to write next. If she could make her parents get a dog, that would be awesome. Or maybe she could publish another poem in *Nic Notes*, the school's literary magazine. That would be satisfying, but it wasn't truly thrilling. If she could write away her dad's aversion to amusement parks, maybe they could take a family trip to Orlando over winter break. J.R. reminded herself to keep an eye out for a suitable cover to make that one possible.

Excited and anxious for Ms. Kline's next assignment, J.R. retrieved her copy of the *Mixed-Up Files* from her room. Since she knew the story by heart, she sometimes picked a random page and started there. With one eye on the TV, J.R. opened to chapter 3, as the Kincaids plan their first night at the museum. Claudia directs her brother to wait in the men's room until the night watchman makes his rounds, which he isn't too thrilled about. Then she finds a beautiful bed for them to sleep in, but her brother doesn't care about a boring old antique, at least until his sister discovers that it was the scene of a sixteenth-century murder. That gets Jamie's attention. Eventually, both siblings begin to appreciate the other's contributions. Claudia, after all, only brought Jamie along so that she could use his allowance. The Kincaids didn't start out united. But as their adventure continues, they get closer and closer. The next line jumped out at J.R.—"What happened was: they became a team, a family of two."

J.R. didn't have any siblings, of course, but she loved the idea of a joint adventure. She wanted to be a team with Violet, one like they used to be. As J.R. reread the line, an idea dawned on her. It was silly to try to write Ava out of the picture. What she needed to do was to write Violet back in, and she didn't want to wait for another assignment to do it.

J.R. leaned over the side of the couch and rustled through her mother's magazine rack until she found what she was looking for: six issues of *Gothamite* that were lying around. J.R. said good night to her father and took the magazines back to her room. As she passed by her parents' bedroom, she heard her mom on the phone.

"I know," Caroline Silver said. "But they've always been so close. I feel like something's going on." J.R. paused outside the door. "No, no. She hasn't said anything, although I'm not sure she would. She's never been much for sharing. Maybe if Violet could invite her along next time—"

A rush of humiliation jolted through J.R. She couldn't believe her mother would talk about her like that, presumably to Violet's mom. And how embarrassing that even her mother thought she needed help managing her friendship. J.R. didn't know if she felt more mad or more humiliated, but the combination was terrible. If her mom actually wanted to help, she could let J.R. go to Wachusett next year. After all, if she had been there last summer, Ava never would have been able to steal her best friend.

Fleeing to her room, J.R. put on her writing outfit and studied the magazine covers while she tried to forget what she had heard. The lights were on below in the garden, and J.R. peeked outside. Alex sat on his wicker couch with a book in his lap and a cocktail glass on the table beside him. It seemed too dark to read, but he looked perfectly comfortable. J.R. saw movement before a mouse ran toward a row of green leafy plants along the back wall. At least it wasn't a rat.

J.R. sat back on her bed and turned to the magazines. On one cover from the end of the summer, a little boy licked an enormous cone of cotton candy as he walked along a board-walk with his dad. From a billboard above, a deeply tanned woman in a bathing suit looked down on the beachgoers with a bottle of tanning oil in her hand and a gauzy look in her eye. The father and son, though, were burned bright pink, pretty much matching the boy's sugary treat. On another, a girl tugged longingly at her mom's arm as they walked by a mobile pet adoption van. J.R. was surprised her mom kept the cover around in light of their family disagreements about getting a pet.

Neither cover helped solve J.R.'s problems with Violet, nor did the next few she flipped through. Finally, she found a good option. For the last magazine in the pile, the artist had painted two girls sitting side by side, arms in the air just past the crest of a roller coaster. Their hair floated up as they headed into a steep drop. Most notable was the size of their smiles, which were enormous. By contrast, the man and woman behind them looked terrified.

J.R. picked up her notebook and began to scribble. *The covers are only meant as inspiration*, Ms. Kline had said with their very first assignment. J.R. took the instructions to heart and figured she had room for creative license.

BEST FRIENDS

"Aaahhh!" the girls screamed as the roller coaster shot down from the top. It made four more trips up and down before they were done, each more exhilarating than the last.

"That was incredible!" Rose said when they got off.

"I can't believe you refused to go!" It had taken some convincing for MJ to get Rose onto the ride. She hated the feeling of falling. Or at least that's what she thought.

The graduation field trip to Carnegie Lake Park was the highlight of the year for sixth graders at Iowa County Middle School. On the next ride over, a group of their classmates waited in line for the bumper cars. They shared a few funnel cakes to pass the time.

"Should we join them?" MJ asked. "They'd probably let us cut." She pointed to the family standing behind the kids they knew.

"One more time just us first?" Rose suggested. Then she held out her pinkie to curl around MJ's, something they'd been doing since they were little. It was their way to celebrate being best friends.

MJ looped her pinkie back around Rose's. "Let's do it," she said before the girls circled back for another ride.

J.R. didn't bother reading through the story. It was hardly inspired, but what did it matter? No one else would see it, and the bones were there. Plus, she wasn't being greedy—Rose didn't propose they *never* join the other kids, just that they not go quite yet. *Let's do it*, she wished. *Let's be best friends again.*

And if J.R. were really lucky, she could recycle the cover and use it twice. Maybe then they really could take that family trip to Orlando.

Chapter 12

NOTHING HAPPENED. IN FACT, WORSE than nothing. Ava came back to school the next day, and J.R. couldn't believe it. Only the night before, she had felt so confident in her ability to write the future she wanted into existence. Why hadn't her amusement park story worked?

To add frustration to disillusion, Ava's return made it hard to share her big news with Violet: The Met was opening for sleepovers. J.R.'s mother told her that morning that the new program was official. A benefit of having a mom who worked in the education office was that she could get J.R. and Violet tickets as soon as they picked a date. It was such a perfect activity that J.R. had ignored the hopeful look in her mom's eye when she had suggested it, unwilling to give her mother credit for getting her and Violet back together, but also unwilling to continue to fret about her mom's desire to do so. The sleepover would be too fun.

When the crowd around Ava finally dispersed after

hearing her tale of sudden illness and woe, J.R. pulled Violet aside. "Guess what?" she asked.

"What?" Adelaide popped up between them. The mockingly curious look on her face was enough to make J.R. cringe. She turned her back on the interloper just slightly.

"My mom said they're going to let kids sleep over at the Met, and she can get us tickets for one of the first sessions."

Adelaide snorted. Violet looked down. J.R. didn't know what to do. She wasn't surprised by Adelaide, but what was up with Violet? They'd dreamed about sleeping over at the museum for years.

"Old news," Adelaide said. "Ava's dad's on the board or something, and he got us tickets for the first sleepover this weekend." Without saying more, she pivoted and headed to her desk.

J.R.'s disappointment stung. "So you're going?" she asked Violet.

"Yeah, but you can come, too. You *should* come. Ava just told me about it on the way upstairs. She has five tickets and she wants to invite you." J.R. wondered who had suggested that invitation. It could have been Ava, but more likely it was Violet. Maybe Violet's mom had even said something to make her do it, after the conversation J.R. had overheard last night. "Seriously," said Violet. "Will you come?"

J.R. wasn't convinced, but how could she refuse? "Sure," she said. "That'll be fun." She repeated the word "fun" in her head, willing the repetition to make it true.

101

To J.R.'s relief, Ms. Kline interrupted their conversation by calling the class to attention so she could return some of their old assignments. "What did you do this weekend?" Ms. Kline asked when she passed back J.R.'s strep throat story. The question sounded more like "What have you done?" J.R. reported on her soccer game and, of course, her goal. "I see," Ms. Kline said, looking at J.R. intently. "Anything else?"

"Nothing interesting," J.R. mustered innocently.

"Are you enjoying this writing unit, J.R.?"

"I think so," she answered.

"And you're staying focused? Giving the stories real thought?"

"Yes, definitely," J.R. said, this time with conviction.

"All right then. Concentrate on your schoolwork, and I think you'll see progress. There are no shortcuts around hard work." Ms. Kline nodded, seemingly satisfied by their exchange. When she walked away, J.R. flipped to the comments on the last page of her story.

J.R.:

You put so many details into this assignment.
I could feel how much the girl's throat
hurt and how unhappy she was. I enjoyed
the voice very much and admire your
ambition. I did think there was a bit of
a shift midway through—you started out

rather amusingly terse and then became somewhat wordy. Let's see how you can shift your imagination on the next assignment, perhaps to a happier place?

J.R. didn't know how to interpret the note. She wondered if her teacher had read her soccer story yet. That one was definitely happier, and hopefully more pleasing. Luckily, an opportunity to do better immediately presented itself. Ms. Kline announced a new *Gothamite* assignment and quickly put out a selection of covers. As she circled the room displaying the pictures, she gave her instructions. "The idea of this exercise is to focus on plot," she said. "Who remembers the parts of a story that we talked about last week?" Ms. Kline moved toward the whiteboard and picked up a marker. "Margaret, what happens at the start of a book?"

"Um," Margaret answered. "The backstory?"

"Close enough. The beginning is where the author sets the scene." Ms. Kline made an X on the board. "What's next? Curtis?"

"The climax?" he answered.

"Before that."

"The tension?"

"You're getting there. The rising action." She wrote and underlined the words on the board. "This is the series of events building toward the climax." Ms. Kline drew a jagged line up to the right, a series of ascending cliffs that peaked and then descended, like the outline of a mountain. She went on to review the falling action and resolution on the far side of the summit, completing the arc of a story. "For this assignment, you can pick any part of the dramatic structure you would like. But whatever section you pick—it could be one, it could be more—I also want you to focus on what your protagonist is doing in that specific moment. Become his or her biggest advocate. Push a little, even if your narrative isn't entirely realistic, and see what you can make the character achieve."

Maybe because the assignment sounded complicated, there was less chaos than usual when Ms. Kline finished giving her instructions and sent the class to make their picks. J.R. easily navigated the room until she found a cover that spoke to her. It was one she remembered, in fact, from the previous year— an Easter egg hunt on a big green lawn. Parents supervised while kids searched for candy. The twist was that the adults had iPads for torsos, and the kids' stomachs were replaced by iPhones. "Our phones are our family these days," her mom had said in a resigned tone when the magazine arrived.

J.R. would definitely be the only one at Ava's sleepover without a phone. Normally she didn't care about that sort of thing too much, but maybe it was time to start caring? Maybe it was silly to be so removed. When Ms. Kline saw J.R.'s choice, her teacher stared at the image.

"Are you sure this is the cover you want?"

"I'm sure," J.R. answered. Her voice didn't waver.

"All right then, it's your choice. But remember what I said. I put a lot of thought into my assignments so you can get something out of them. Be sure you do the same."

J.R. mulled over her story all day. In fact, she couldn't stop thinking about it—the last one and the next one, too. Why hadn't anything happened from her roller coaster story? Ms. Kline's cryptic comment kept coming back to her: "Concentrate on your schoolwork, and I think you'll see progress." Was that what had gone wrong? Was it because the story wasn't an actual assignment, just something she had written with one of her mom's magazines? That hunch made J.R. all the more anxious to get started on her homework.

There was still time on the way home to stop into June's, though. Alex had been away for a few days visiting his sister, so J.R. hadn't seen him since she had last gone by with Violet. As she entered the store, a man was leaving. "Thanks again for these," he said to Alex. He flashed a couple of sports books from the early reader section. "I'll be back on Sunday."

Alex wished him a good week and welcomed J.R., who asked about his trip.

"It was really great, actually. Thank you for asking. I hadn't seen my sister in quite a while, and we had a nice time catching up. How about you? Did you have a good weekend?" J.R. told him about her goal, and Alex brought out a blue tin of butter cookies from the back to celebrate. "How're you going to top that next weekend?" he asked as they munched. "It'll be tough!"

More than tough, J.R. thought. Then she found herself talking. She started with how she loved the Met, and how awesome it was that they were going to let kids sleep over. That led her to Ava's invitation, and how J.R. had wanted to go just with Violet. It felt like her plan had somehow been stolen.

"Aren't you being a little unfair?" Alex asked between bites. "It's nice of the girl to invite you, and it's something you want to do. Maybe it'll be like *Night at the Museum* and one of the knights in armor will chase after you, or a mummy will come to life." J.R. scowled at the not-funny joke. Despite his corny humor, though, she found Alex pretty easy to talk to. "Just try it," he encouraged. "Besides, Violet will be there. I remember you two coming in here for story hour when you were little. It was good to see her the other day. I feel like she hasn't been by for a while."

J.R. couldn't tell where Alex was going with his observation. It didn't actually sound like he was fishing for information, but it wasn't the most natural comment, either. J.R. was tempted to say more. With her mom now consumed by work at the office, and without Violet around, she realized how quiet her afternoons had become. She didn't think she liked it, but she didn't really want to talk about that, either.

"Maybe you're right," she said instead. "I mean, I'm going, so I may as well have fun."

What J.R. didn't tell Alex was that she had an idea for how to improve the sleepover, or at least how she could fit in better with Violet's new friends. When she got home, she slipped on her headband, dug out her slippers from under her bed, and carried her notebook to the kitchen table. After slathering slices of apple with peanut butter, she got down to work. There was no need to look at her *Gothamite* cover. She remembered what she needed. Scraping a piece of nut off the roof of her mouth with her tongue, J.R. started to write.

ME INCLUDED

"They're addictive," Mom said. "I can't put down my own phone. How will you stop looking at yours?"

"I promise I'll do it," I told her. "I'll keep it in the kitchen at night, and I can't use it at school. That's sixteen hours right there you don't need to worry about. You can even set one of those timers that locks me out."

I knew the drill on all the parental controls. My friends had suffered through them already. But the class consensus was that adults gave up on monitoring pretty quickly. After all, who would want to read a lot of sixth graders' texts?

"I just don't think it's a good idea. There's so much inappropriate content on the internet. All that—" Mom stopped herself. I didn't want to think about the end of that sentence.

"Mom, I know you say plenty of other kids don't have a phone, and I know you don't want to hear the list of kids that do."

"Who do," she corrected me. It was a struggle, but I managed to stop myself from rolling my eyes.

"There are barely any of us without one." I paused to muster my argument. I decided to lay it on pretty thick. "It means I feel left out. I don't get their jokes. I'm never tagged in photos or invited to parties. I'm not included. Even my best friend is leaving me behind."

J.R. put down her pen for a second as the action rose. What she was writing was sort of true but definitely exaggerated. It wasn't like *everyone* in sixth grade had a phone. And she did feel left out, sometimes, although she wasn't particularly sure the things she was left out of were things she wanted to do. It was more that she was curious. Her mom wouldn't be sympathetic to arguments about who had what, or what J.R. thought she should get. But she did seem to worry about J.R.'s feelings. She might be too worried these days, in fact. If she was going to worry so much that she had to talk to Violet's mom about it, J.R. felt justified in using that maternal concern to her advantage.

The action climaxed.

> Mom looked at me for a second before she responded. "I know it's hard being in sixth grade," she said. "And I don't want to make it harder. But I'm still the parent, and we're going to have rules."

That last part was an actual line J.R.'s dad had used once when her grandparents gave her a hamster without consulting her parents first. The aforementioned rules—mainly that J.R. had to feed her pet and clean the cage—hadn't lasted long. Neither had the hamster.

> Mom proceeded with her list: "No phone in your room when you're trying to sleep. No phones at the dinner table, of course."
>
> "No problem," I said, so quickly my mom got annoyed. She wasn't done.
>
> "If you abuse your privileges, you'll lose your phone until you prove you deserve to get it back."
>
> "I got it, Mom. Thank you!" I gave her a huge hug.

J.R. read over her story, from the rising action through the end. Now what she needed was a real-life resolution.

Chapter 13

J.R. WOKE UP THE NEXT morning to a familiar noise. It sounded exactly like her father's alarm, his phone alarm specifically. J.R. squeezed her eyes shut, trying to will her story into being with the force of her eyelids.

"Surprise!" her parents said in unison, bursting into her room. "Happy half birthday!"

The Silvers hadn't celebrated J.R.'s half birthday since she was three, or three and a half, to be precise. She hadn't even thought about reaching the halfway mark for years, but now that her parents mentioned it, perhaps that had been an opportunity lost. "Is that?" J.R. asked, pointing to a phone sitting on top of her nightstand without daring to say the words out loud.

"All yours," her mom answered. "We set it up for you last night."

J.R. gently picked up the phone for inspection. Her parents had even set the wallpaper with a photo from their summer trip to Maine. "Thank you!" she said, studying the picture.

They surely assumed that the gift was the entire source of her delight. What they couldn't know was that she was equally happy, if not more so, to know that things were back in action. Her last story had clearly produced results. Under normal, non-magazine circumstances, her parents would never have simply bought her a phone. J.R. wanted to squeal, but she stopped herself. That would have been too much.

"Be careful, please," her dad cautioned. "Kids do dumb things with those, you know? I don't want you to start worrying about what other people are doing all the time because you see pictures they post, and don't write something you wouldn't want someone to write about you."

"Dad," J.R. groaned. Her father had a way of jumping into serious mode. "You shouldn't stress," she assured him. "I barely know how to use this thing, anyway."

She learned fast, though. After school that day, Violet added her to the sixth-grade group chat. It opened up a whole new world. J.R. had no idea how many kids didn't like their science teacher or were genuinely worried about the math test on Friday. She definitely hadn't realized how late some of her classmates stayed up. In the Silver household, all phones lived in the kitchen overnight. When they checked in the morning, J.R. always had way more new messages than her parents.

Violet opened an Instagram account for her, too, telling J.R. not to worry about the fact that she wasn't really thirteen. Everyone just pretended. Now J.R. could see the pictures Adelaide posted of her bedroom, which was pink, and her mother's bathroom, which was pinker. She saw Ava's dog again, and again, and again. He got her a lot of likes. Curtis posted about a million pictures of his flag football team. Even Tommy was on Instagram. He wasn't exaggerating when he said he spent a lot of time with his cousin. Violet posted, too, although not that often and mostly pictures of her with her orchestra. She got tagged in a lot of photos, though, with Ava, Aria, and Adelaide.

For everything J.R. saw on her phone, she mostly just observed. Sometimes she liked a post or texted Violet, but she never posted her own pictures or commented on the group chat.

"You can't lurk and never say anything," Violet warned after a couple of days. "People will think you're weird."

J.R. wondered if Violet really meant to use the future tense, or if people already thought she was odd. She vowed to weigh in sometime, but she could never quite figure out what to say. Of course, J.R. actually had news that was way more interesting than anything her classmates had to share, but for some unspoken reason, she knew her secret had to be protected. It was definitely exciting, though.

By Saturday, when it was time for the Met sleepover, J.R. had almost convinced herself she really would have a good time. At least she put on a good face when her mom dropped her off.

"I'm jealous!" her mother said as they passed the fountains in front of the museum. "I wish I could join you." She meant to be encouraging, but J.R. felt bad. Her mom probably did want to spend the night at the Met, unlike Ava's older sister, who had been sent to chaperone as punishment for sneaking out of their apartment.

Inside the museum, the guests gathered by the base of the stairs at the back of the Great Hall. J.R. found her group easily after Violet gave her a big, giddy wave that made her Met button earrings bounce. J.R. felt herself relax a little to see Violet wearing them. A woman with a clipboard started directing groups to the galleries where they were going to sleep. The plan was to find their cots and leave their things, and then they were going on a scavenger hunt. Ava's sister checked her paperwork and located their sleeping assignment: the Damascus Room.

"That's awesome!" Violet said. Adelaide mimicked her silently but not subtly.

The Damascus Room was a winter sitting area from a wealthy Syrian family's home. It was about three hundred years old and had elaborate wood panels on the walls and shelves holding blue-and-white pottery. The ceiling was also made out of carved wood, and windows on the left side were lit brightly from behind to make it look like the sun was shining in. J.R. imagined there was a beautiful courtyard out there that she couldn't quite see, since visitors weren't allowed past the fountain at the front. The room was one of her and Violet's mutual favorites—it was lucky they got assigned to that spot. It felt like fate.

"So it's a good one?" Ava asked enthusiastically.

"Totally," said Violet. "But it's got a marble floor with mosaics. I can't believe we can actually sleep there."

A nearby docent overheard. "You're right," she chimed in cheerfully. "We couldn't get you that close, but the cots are in the gallery just in front. If you grab your bags, I'll take you." The woman looked kind of familiar, and J.R. hoped that if she worked with her mom, she wouldn't say anything. J.R. didn't need to be the one kid whose parents came up in conversation. After gathering another group of visitors, the docent led the way to the Damascus Room. There were nine cots laid out in two rows, and two more placed one gallery over for the chaperones.

"I call this one," Adelaide said, picking the bed at the center of the front row closest to the roped-off room. "Guest of honor next to me!" She beckoned Ava to the bed beside her.

"It's all right," Ava said happily. "I'll go here." She was already standing by the cot at the end. Violet sat down between Ava and Adelaide, who looked miffed. Adelaide quickly grabbed Aria's arm and pulled her toward the bed on her other side, leaving one cot on the far end of the row for J.R. The other four girls assigned to the room, who were only about seven years old, took the line of beds behind them. They were chattering away in two groups of two.

"Say cheese!" Adelaide said, backing up against the wall for a better angle. She posted the photo immediately, muttering their names one by one as she tagged them. "Ava, Aria, Violet," she said, then stopped. "Oops!" she added. "I almost forgot J.R.'s on here now." J.R. smiled as if the comment was funny. "I recognize that sweatshirt," Adelaide said when she finished taking pictures. J.R. silently thanked her grandmother for picking out the blue hoodie with fuzzy lining, which had been a back-to-school gift. She was better than J.R.'s mom when it came to things like that. "My sister has the same one," Adelaide continued. "She's six, though."

"Well, I think it looks good," Violet interjected before J.R.'s heart could totally sink. Violet gave Aria her phone and wrapped her arm around J.R. "Take one of us?" The two girls smiled, but J.R. noticed that Violet put the phone back in her bag without posting.

After they unpacked, the docent announced it was time for the scavenger hunt. "Please be sure to take any valuables with you," she said. "The museum's only responsible for our own." No one laughed at the joke. When everyone pulled out their phone, J.R. was glad to be able to get hers out, too.

The docent separated Ava's friends from the younger girls and handed out a list of clues. They had one hour to answer the questions, and the chaperones were supposed to take a picture of the group in front of each room or object they identified. "One other thing," the docent concluded. "Bring your valuables, but don't use them. Explore the museum and have fun, but no Googling. Also, for some of the clues there is more than one right answer."

Violet looked at J.R. expectantly. "We've got this, right?"

"Right."

According to the instructions, they needed a team name and mascot to start.

"How about Louis for the mascot?" Violet offered.

"Sounds good to me," Aria chimed in.

J.R. couldn't disagree. She had never actually met Ava's puppy, but she felt like she knew him from all the pictures.

"Louis's Treasure Hunters," Ava wrote on the top of the sheet, taking charge and extrapolating from their agreement on the mascot to a team name. It didn't have much of a ring to it, but J.R. was ready to get going and was glad not to get bogged down in debate. She listened to Ava read the first clue: "Where would I be if I see swans swimming in water?"

"The Tiffany mosaic!" J.R. called out. "You know, the one in the American Wing that's pastel-colored and gold, with the fountain in front?"

"I don't know the one, but that sounds good to me." Ava looked to Violet to confirm.

"Definitely," Violet said. She led the way through the Greek and Roman sculptures, then past European Paintings and down the stairs to the first floor of the American Wing. Besides Ava's sister and a guard assigned to trail their group, no one else was there. The team gathered around for a picture to prove they'd solved the clue.

Ava read the second prompt: "A famous American architect designed this nearby space for a house in the Land of 10,000 Lakes."

"I know that one!" Aria said. "It's the Frank Lloyd Wright Room we saw on that field trip last year." J.R. was moderately impressed. The girls crossed the atrium and took another photo. It was a cool space, J.R. thought, but for a family room it didn't look very family friendly. With all the wood and glass and lack of stuff, it felt sterile. J.R. definitely could not imagine a stack of board games or a pile of to-be-folded laundry in the space, never mind a TV. Even her neat-freak father would have a hard time living up to Wright's standards.

The hunt continued, bringing them next to "the most famous dancer in the museum." They all knew that one—it was a bronze sculpture by Edgar Degas of a ballerina with a real silk tutu. It was harder to come up with something for "the creepiest hair" until J.R. remembered seeing a poster for a special exhibit on Medusa. That earned her praise from everyone but Adelaide, although silence was preferable to cutting comments. As she spent more time with Violet's new friends, J.R. realized they weren't quite as alike as she had thought, nor were they as unified. As if on cue, when Ava read out the next clue, "The embodiment of four seasons," Adelaide snorted.

"What?" Ava was clearly annoyed.

"Kind of dramatic, don't you think?" There was a defensive note in Adelaide's voice, like just maybe she wished she could take the snort back.

"I think it sounds romantic," Ava countered. By sticking with her own convictions, she inspired J.R. to back her up.

"I agree, and I know what it is. I bet Violet does, too."

"Haverhill Room?" Violet asked.

"Haverhill Room," J.R. answered. Then they guided the group back to the American Wing, past the bank facade at the far side of the main courtyard, and into the period rooms, where they located four one-foot-tall porcelain figurines above the Haverhill Room's fireplace. Each one personified a season. "I like *Winter*," J.R. explained, pointing to the doll with her hands in a muff, "and Violet's favorite is *Spring*." That one held a garland of flowers.

"And that's J.R.'s favorite bed in the whole museum," Violet said, turning to the white canopied furniture.

"Cool!" Ava said. "Like from the *Mixed-Up Files*?"

J.R.'s momentary instinct was to balk, but to her surprise, without even trying, it faded. She was glad Ava recognized the connection to the book. The scavenger hunt was proving to be fun, and J.R. almost forgot she hadn't wanted to come. Eventually they got to the second-to-last clue, Big Bird's temple.

"Huh?" Adelaide scrunched up her nose. "Big Bird from *Sesame Street*?"

"Don't worry, J.R. and I've got this one," Violet assured her.

"I knew there was a reason you were invited."

"What did you say?" All the girls froze, even Ava's sister. Tension between Ava and Adelaide had been escalating, and there was no mistaking Ava's tone. She wasn't happy.

"I just said I knew it was good they were invited," Adelaide said in a saccharine voice that no one could have mistaken for genuinely sweet. "J.R. and Violet have been here, like, a million times. Right?"

"I guess I must have heard wrong." Ava clearly didn't think she had misheard. "But we agree, then. I'm glad we have some experts in our group." Ava and Adelaide looked at each other. J.R. looked at the ground, both embarrassed and impressed.

"So what do you think this Big Bird clue is about?" Ava asked Violet, breaking the spell.

"There was an old *Sesame Street* movie where all the characters got locked in the Met overnight, and Big Bird helped free the ghost of an Egyptian boy who was trapped in the museum. I think the temple is the Temple of Dendur."

"We know the Temple of Dendur," said Adelaide in a snarky tone. Apparently, it didn't matter that Ava had just put her in her place. Or maybe that had made things worse. "The Temple of Dendur is, like, the most famous thing here."

Violet didn't bother to respond. Instead, she just headed toward the ancient temple at the northern end of the museum. When they reached the huge hall that housed the stone building, two other groups were there already and two more arrived at the same time. They must have all had the Big Bird clue on their list. Ava's group gathered in front of the stone steps, and her sister took a picture.

There was one last question to answer. "What's the best view in the house?" Ava read.

"Huh?" said Aria. "I mean, that one's pretty good." She pointed to the enormous outer wall of the room. It was made entirely of glass and angled inward like the side of a pyramid. The window looked out over Central Park, although by then all they could see were a few lights illuminating the paths and the headlights from some cars.

"That is a good one," Ava agreed. "What about the view from the top of the balcony around the entrance hall?"

"Or what's up there?" Adelaide pointed before Ava finished talking. Everyone followed her finger to the top of the back wall, a huge swath of light-colored stone with one square glass window in the upper left corner, almost near the ceiling. "That room must have an awesome view."

That, J.R. knew, was true. The gallery that Adelaide didn't know she was pointing to was tiny and wood-paneled, with benches topped by tatami mats lining two of the walls. In the middle stood a taxidermy deer nicknamed Bubbles, on account of the fact that it was covered in clear glass globes of all different sizes, antlers included. Bubbles's Bedroom, as J.R. and Violet called it, was home to the best place to sit in the whole museum, the corner of the bench on the back wall. From there they could look one way at Bubbles—modern, Japanese, and more than a little bit silly—and another out the window that overlooked the Temple of Dendur one very high-ceilinged floor below. Somehow, there weren't a lot of people who found the room when wandering through the Asian Art galleries, and seemingly no one got curious looking up from below and decided to go find it. It was the museum's best-kept secret, at least until now.

"It does have an awesome view."

J.R. couldn't believe it. Why would Violet say that, especially to Adelaide, who was being a brat? "I don't think—" J.R. said.

"What?" Violet cut her off.

What could she say? *I don't think it does? I don't think we should go up there? I don't think they'll like it? I don't want to share?*

"Want me to show you?" Violet asked before J.R. could say anything. There was a hint of a challenge in her voice.

"Sure," Adelaide answered.

Violet marched the group upstairs, weaving past Egyptian artifacts and Chinese scrolls until they got to the Japanese galleries.

"Gross," Aria proclaimed when they reached their destination. As usual, there was no one else there.

"I think it looks cool." Ava took a selfie as the girls circled Bubbles. They peered through the translucent globes, which magnified the fur underneath if they looked toward the deer at one angle or distorted what was on the wall behind the sculpture if they looked from another. J.R. hung back.

"It looks like it has a disease," Adelaide said.

"But it's kind of awesome," Ava countered.

J.R. cringed. She knew she shouldn't feel this way, but the fact that Ava appreciated Bubbles made things worse.

"I don't like looking at that thing," said Adelaide. "But I definitely found us the best view." She took Aria and Ava by the hand and pulled them over to the window, where they stared down at the Temple of Dendur. J.R. stood at the gallery entrance waiting for everyone to finish. Violet came over, looking a little sheepish.

"What's up? You didn't want to see Bubbles?" Violet

definitely knew that wasn't really the issue. J.R. shrugged. If she forced herself to speak up, J.R. wondered if Violet would admit they shouldn't be there, but neither of them spoke. Eventually her friend said, "Let's get going." Then, more loudly to the group, with what sounded like forced cheer, "I think our time's up. This is our pick for best view, right?"

"I vote yes," said Aria.

"Me too," said Ava.

"Fine with me," Adelaide added.

Violet turned to J.R. "Do you agree?"

You know I do, J.R. thought. Instead, she said, "I do." Then the five girls clustered together with Bubbles, and Ava's sister took a picture.

With their scavenger hunt finished, the group headed back to the Damascus Room. A new docent showed them the bathroom where they could change and brush their teeth. J.R. finished first and went back to her cot. She pulled out her phone and scrolled through the photos Ava had already posted. It made her kind of proud to be in them.

When the other girls came back, Ava and Violet both wore big Wachusett T-shirts on top of flannel pants. J.R. must have looked unintentionally sad because Violet said, "You'll be there next summer, too, right? I'm sure we can convince your parents this time." J.R. wasn't so sure, but she smiled.

The girls all lay down on their cots, and the docent dimmed the lights. She told them to whisper if they wanted to talk. That's when J.R. realized just how weird it was to be in the museum at night. Even with the quiet voices, the loudest noise in the room was the gurgling fountain.

"That was really fun," Aria said to J.R. from the next cot over.

"What'd you say?" It would have been a stretch to call Adelaide's voice a whisper.

"I said that was fun," Aria repeated.

"I guess." From the other side of the room, Violet laughed at something J.R. couldn't hear. "Doesn't it bug you?" Adelaide asked.

"What?" J.R. asked.

"The way Violet ditched you. It's like she'd do anything to be friends with Ava."

"Come on, Adelaide," Aria said quietly.

"I'm just saying."

Saying what? J.R. wondered. After all, Adelaide was getting ditched just like she was. Rather than answer, J.R. rolled over and pretended to go to sleep. The rest of the girls whispered for a long time until eventually the room was silent. Then J.R.'s phone buzzed.

How is it? Tommy texted.

How's what?

The sleepover! I saw Ava's pictures. Are you having fun?

J.R. thought about her answer. Not sure, she finally typed.

Understood, came the response.

Chapter 14

"I MEAN, THAT WAS PRETTY great," Violet said on Monday between mouthfuls of cheese and avocado sandwich in the cafeteria. She and Ava had declared themselves vegetarians while at camp. When school first started, J.R. felt self-conscious eating the turkey on wheat bread with a tiny swirl of yellow mustard that she made every day at the sandwich bar. But she decided pretty quickly that she liked what she liked, or more precisely, that her capacity to sweat the small stuff was in fact finite. Worrying about sandwich choices crossed a line.

"What was pretty great, Fernando?" Curtis asked with his mouth full as he walked to the silverware trays. His smell lingered behind him. All sixth graders had PE twice a week before lunch, which was only borderline acceptable as far as hygiene went, especially since some of the boys had yet to embrace deodorant.

"None of your business," J.R. snapped. Her tone got the

attention of several classmates, but Curtis just swallowed his food and kept walking. He called a lot of boys by their last names, but she had never heard him do it to a girl, never mind Violet. She also didn't need him interrupting. Half the class was away on a science field trip to the American Museum of Natural History, including Ava, Aria, and Adelaide. All J.R. wanted was to enjoy lunch in peace. "I agree," she said, turning back to Violet. "It was so cool to sleep there."

The more she thought about the sleepover, the more J.R. realized she had genuinely had fun. It was a thrill to have the place to themselves, and she knew she really had helped her team complete the scavenger hunt.

J.R. made a purposeful decision to focus on the positive. Halloween was only a few weeks away, and they hadn't even talked about costumes. Every year, Violet and J.R. went to Taylor's Toys to pick them out. "Should we go to Taylor's this weekend?" she asked.

"Oh." Violet looked uncomfortable. They were sitting at the end of a table near the water dispenser, and Violet got up to refill her cup. She took a long sip, then sat back down. "I kind of told Ava I'd go with her."

"When?" J.R. asked. Ava's inclusion was hardly good news, but in the spirit of being positive she tried to stay calm. Maybe it wouldn't be so bad to all go together.

"Last night," Violet said, misunderstanding the question. "Do you want to coordinate with us, and Adelaide and Aria, too?"

J.R. glanced down at her sandwich, which suddenly looked distinctly unappetizing. She wondered why Violet had agreed to go shopping with Ava at all, never mind with the other two girls. But how should she ask without sounding hurt or, even worse, embarrassed about being left out?

"It'll be fun," Violet continued with a hint of pleading. Maybe she felt guilty about abandoning J.R. or worried that her mom would be mad at her for doing it. Or maybe Violet really wanted her to join. "You'd like those girls if you gave them a chance." Now her tone was more defiant. "Or at least you'd like Ava." J.R. smiled, just a little. It was a small consolation that Violet hadn't given a full seal of approval to Adelaide and Aria quite yet. "I think it would be good if we did stuff with other people more, you know?"

"Yeah, of course." J.R. forced the smile to stay in place, which took all the cheek muscles she had.

"There are actually some pretty cool kids in our class who I hadn't really talked to before."

J.R. wondered who Violet had in mind besides her new trio of friends. Could Violet really even be part of her adopted group, since her name didn't start with A? Rather than ask, J.R. nodded her head and did her best to look convincing. Even when she tried, though, she couldn't actually think of anyone else she wanted to hang out with. Not that Violet was her only friend, but she was her best friend, and that was all she needed. "I guess I'll think about Halloween," she said.

"Great!" Violet sounded genuinely excited. "But think

quickly because we want to get costumes soon. We're thinking of going as zombie pop stars."

Right before dismissal and after the other half of the class was back from their field trip, Ms. Kline announced it was time for their next *Gothamite* assignment. "Tonight you're going to work on dialogue," she said. "You don't need to bother with extraneous details; just focus on what two characters are saying and how they say it. Your reader will get lost in your story if the conversation sounds like one that could happen in real life rather than something stilted on the page. Remember that no two people sound exactly alike, so you need to differentiate between your characters."

"Not even Aria and Adelaide," Margaret mumbled under her breath.

"Finally, in your composition I would like one of the people to take a risk."

"Like a girl asking the coolest boy in the grade out on a date," Curtis joked. "Will he say yes, or will he say no? Sounds risky."

"That wouldn't have been my example, but if you find that compelling, Curtis, please go right ahead. Each of you should be growing through these assignments, but everyone's experience as a writer will not be the same."

"Sounds sappy," Carlos said to Tommy, who shrugged.

J.R.'s ears perked up. She hoped her teacher might say

more on the topic of experiencing the assignments differently, but of course she didn't.

"There's one more thing," Ms. Kline went on. "All of you must include at least one direct question in your story that elicits a direct answer. Keep it short and simple."

How typical of her teacher to end on an odd note. J.R. started to think of questions she wanted to know the answer to. *May I have a puppy?* remained near the top of the list, although Ms. Kline never put out the right cover for that. The more serious question remained, of course, *Are we still best friends?* That was the one she wanted to ask Violet, and the question she really wanted answered.

And that was when J.R. saw the perfect cover. It showed a crowd of people gathered on the front steps of the Met on a bright summer day. Most of them were regular visitors, probably tourists. But mixed into the scene were Frida Kahlo and Diego Rivera strolling arm in arm, Vincent van Gogh—recognizable by his beard and missing ear—ordering from a hot dog cart, and an ancient Egyptian mummy walking stiffly toward the door. "I love it!" Adelaide said as she picked up the drawing.

"No!" Aria and Adelaide looked at J.R. She made herself continue even though she had to force more words out of her mouth, and not very articulate ones at that. "Sorry, I mean, I really had my heart set on that one. Do you think we could trade?"

Can we trade? J.R. silently rephrased the rambling question

130

into a simple sentence. How come she could never be direct when it really mattered?

"But you don't have anything to trade for it." Aria pointed to J.R.'s empty hands.

"I really love this one," Adelaide said. "Sorry, but I want to keep it." She didn't look sorry at all.

"It's actually kind of important to me." J.R. could hear the desperation in her voice and didn't like it. But she made a decision to press on. Something told her she needed that cover. Violet had clearly had fun during the scavenger hunt. Maybe J.R. could re-create one? Or maybe there was something else they could do at the Met. The *Mixed-Up Files* wasn't simply a book about running away; it was a story about how Jamie and Claudia Kincaid come together to solve a mystery—whether Michelangelo had sculpted a beautiful statue that the museum recently acquired. Maybe J.R. could write a mystery for her and Violet to solve. A lot of things seemed possible if she could just get that magazine.

"The cover's important to you?" Adelaide asked, snapping J.R. back to the present while Adelaide examined the image. "That's weird. Maybe Ms. Kline will put it out again next time."

"Do you think you could use it next time?" J.R. made her voice as polite as possible.

"I don't know. What's so important?" Adelaide's tone softened, like she was actually considering the trade.

"I guess I just like it. And—" J.R. wondered if an appeal to what she suspected was unspoken common ground of strained friendship just might work. "It reminds me of lots of my trips to the museum with Violet."

Adelaide studied J.R. Then she looked at Violet and Ava, who were admiring a picture of a string quartet playing on an empty beach beneath a lone palm tree. Wearing tattered clothes, the musicians appeared to have been there a while.

"It looks like Violet's moved on," Adelaide said in a whisper, her eyes trained on the two girls. "So I think I'll keep it."

As J.R. followed Adelaide's gaze toward Violet and Ava, she absorbed the double sting of the truth of Adelaide's words and the loss of the cover. A dull ache in her eyes turned to a burn. Wanting to get away before wiping any tears, J.R. resumed her search. At the same time, Ms. Kline clapped three times to hurry the class along.

Having lost hope, J.R. took the next cover she saw. She must have missed it at home, because it was dated the week before. The picture showed a young couple standing next to a jack-o'-lantern outside their door. The woman held a baby dressed as a watermelon, and the man held a bowl of candy as he watched a group of trick-or-treaters depart. At the back of the line, last to leave, a tall, skinny man wearing a burglar's black eye mask and carrying an overflowing sack on his shoulder munched on a mini candy. A trail of jewelry and electronics littered the ground behind him. Despite herself, J.R. laughed. If she had been the artist, J.R. would have added an old-fashioned portrait to his loot, like the burglar had plucked it off a wall, too, under the cover of Halloween chaos.

The Halloween humor broke her funk and triggered her curiosity. If she wanted to get to the bottom of things, she had to talk to Ms. Kline. Everything inexplicable revolved around her teacher's magazines, and J.R. was pretty sure Ms. Kline knew more than she was letting on. It wouldn't be easy to get information out of her— that wasn't Ms. Kline's style. Nor was it J.R.'s style to press. Maybe she needed to change that.

Chapter 15

WHEN SCHOOL ENDED FOR THE day, J.R. left with the Walkers, then circled back to the hallway outside room 602. "May I please talk to you, Ms. Kline?" she repeated over and over in her head to build courage. It was harder to decide where to go from there. J.R. silently tried out potential next lines.

"Is there something I should know about these magazine assignments?"

"Has anyone reported anything weird about the *Gothamite* covers before?"

"When I make things up on paper, they somehow become true."

"What is going on?!"

As J.R. kept going, Ms. Kline failed to reappear from dismissing the Greeters. J.R. eventually let herself back into the classroom. The floor below her seat was still sticky with orange juice Margaret had spilled that morning, so J.R. went to Ms. Kline's desk to wait. There by the filing cabinet filled with *Gothamite* covers, her curiosity got the better of her. J.R. knew she shouldn't do it, but she pulled open the top drawer. A folder at the front with just one page inside caught her attention. J.R. wanted to look away but she couldn't. She took out the folder and removed the letter, which was written in impeccable handwriting on a piece of pale blue paper.

Dear Kate,

On the eve of my retirement, I have enjoyed reflecting on my years of teaching and the many remarkable students I've met, some more remarkable than others.

There is a lot at stake, as you can imagine, in deciding what to do with the magazines, but I've made my decision and I am giving them to you. I know your teaching career is just getting started, but I am confident you will be an exceptional steward, and it takes a certain strength, which you have, to move around so often. I was rarely lonely, but remember there is always a member of the alumni network nearby if you need a friend—someone summoned you there, after all.

Go with your instincts when picking your secondments and be sure to visit some wonderful places (I particularly enjoyed

Honolulu, Hawaii, and Bozeman, Montana).
There are always more needs to meet, so you
really do have to keep moving. Usually, it
takes 8 to 10 assignments to ignite change. I
find poetry works well toward the end, when
students have a better handle on language.
Food for thought when planning your syllabus.

I know the collection intimately by now and
have organized it by year. You may find,
especially early on, that thematic folders are
more efficient. You'll quickly learn which images
are most impactful. Friendship, empathy, sports,
and pets will all be in heavy rotation.

A teacher's work is never done, but it is
usually a pleasure. You are going to make a
real difference. I see your spark.

Most fondly,
Eleanor Mendell

J.R. held the note carefully and scanned through it a second
time. Most of the information wasn't new; Ms. Kline had told
the whole class that she inherited the magazines from her own
sixth-grade teacher. But what did Ms. Mendell mean about the
images having impact, and what were these secondments Ms.
Kline would pick? Was J.R.'s school one of them? The alumni
network she mentioned caught J.R.'s attention, too, although

she had no idea what to make of it. J.R. wanted answers, but getting caught with the letter in hand would not help her get them. She gently placed the note back in the folder and shut the drawer. Then she walked around to the opposite side of Ms. Kline's desk, where a form caught her attention just as her teacher arrived. It said "Columbia Teachers College Letter of Reference" at the top.

"Hello, J.R. Were you looking for me?" Ms. Kline was truly the master of impassive expressions.

J.R. was unable to maintain similar calm, forgetting instantly about the reference form. "I have a question about our writing assignments," she blurted out.

Ms. Kline took a seat at her desk. She did not motion for J.R. to sit down. "And what is your question, exactly?"

If J.R. stopped to think, she would lose her nerve. "I came to talk about the *Gothamite* assignments. You've said that I should focus on bringing the images to life. I'm not sure what you mean exactly." J.R. wanted to kick herself. That wasn't really her question.

"I mean just that." Ms. Kline sat up so straight it must have made her back hurt. "I mean you should write details into your work so that a vivid story emerges. What would you want to happen, even if you can't imagine it really happening? The more you push yourself, the more you'll get out of your writing."

"Actually, I feel like I'm getting a lot out of my writing already. Maybe more than you would expect?" J.R. waited but Ms. Kline did not react. "I've noticed—"

"I wasn't quite finished." Ms. Kline's speech was as sharp as her posture, and she pronounced every word in a staccato. "You're a promising writer, but dialogue sometimes gives you trouble. My advice would be to read what you write out loud. Ask yourself how it sounds. Imagine what you, J.R., would say if you were the one having the conversation. Imagine what you *could* say, and let the story give you the space to say it."

"I can try that." J.R. fidgeted. It was weird to be standing over Ms. Kline, but no invitation to sit had materialized. "I've noticed, though—"

"Yes?"

It seemed so ridiculous, J.R. almost couldn't get the words out. "I think I've noticed that when I write these stories, the things I write come true. Sometimes."

Ms. Kline's eyelids fluttered. J.R. wondered if she was going to close them altogether. "Do you remember what I told you about shortcuts?"

J.R. thought before answering. "That they won't work?"

"Precisely. And remember what I told you to focus on?" J.R. drew a momentary blank before Ms. Kline answered her own question. "Your assignments. Not, for example, your creative writing endeavors at home. So where does that leave us?"

Even more confused? J.R. said to herself. But in truth, she didn't feel entirely confused. She felt like her sneaking suspicion was about to be confirmed. J.R. took a deep breath and then asked, "So I'm right, then? When I write the *Gothamite* stories, I'm making things come true?"

"You are."

"But it has to be for an assignment? I can't use a magazine from home?"

"That's correct." Ms. Kline's face was as neutral as her answer.

The same was not true for J.R. Now she was beaming. At the rate Ms. Kline handed out assignments, that restriction hardly felt limiting. More importantly, the magic was real. "This is so amazing!" J.R. gushed. "I mean, it's incredible. I can't believe it. Or I can believe it, I guess, because I kept thinking it was happening. But it seemed so improbable. Magic magazines?" The words came out faster and faster. "I mean," she said again, "that's so cool! I can do anything!"

"J.R., please. Slow down." The teacher modeled her request by speaking slowly herself. "You cannot, I'm afraid, simply do anything. There are limits." J.R. waited to hear what those limits were, but instead her teacher changed the subject. "You remind me a lot of myself when I was young. It was hard, at first, to comprehend what the magazines meant, or what I was supposed to do with them. It's so tempting, I know, to want to try everything and use them as a magic wand. But this isn't a game, it's work. And you need to be thoughtful."

"It feels like a game," J.R. squealed.

Ms. Kline held up her hand in full stop. Now her expression was not neutral but stern. "With every story, you're changing fate. You got a free pass with your first one. The walking home was rather clever. But after that, with the good comes the bad. So be careful what you write, and be careful what you wish for." J.R. drew back. "Most importantly, keep pushing yourself. I promise you will have plenty of opportunities. It's up to you to take them."

Ms. Kline appeared to be done, but J.R. still had questions. "What about everyone else? Am I the only one who's getting these...opportunities?" It wasn't quite the right word, but a better one eluded her.

"You are the only one in our class," her teacher said.

"Why me?"

"Because someone noticed that you have something to say, but you're struggling to say it. And that someone called me." J.R. wanted to ask if that someone was a member of the alumni network Ms. Mendell had mentioned, but asking would reveal that she had read the letter. "You're doing well, J.R. I think you're getting there."

With that, Ms. Kline rose from her chair and started putting papers into a big black bag that was already crammed full. J.R. stood still and hoped Ms. Kline would keep talking, but she didn't. After a few more seconds of silent disbelief, she mumbled goodbye and stepped toward the door. Her head was spinning.

Chapter 16

By THE TIME SHE MADE it home from practice, J.R. was still digesting the day. Clanging pots and pans suggested her parents were cooking dinner. J.R. called out hello and went straight to her room, where she got out her notebook along with her writing headband. After she peeled off her socks and tossed them in the hamper, her feet were still too sweaty for her usual slippers. She peeked outside, but there was no sign of Alex.

J.R. flopped down on her bed. Now she knew for sure that she was responsible for earning the right to walk home alone, giving Ava strep throat, scoring a winning goal, and getting herself a phone, all with the stroke of a pen. J.R. had always liked that expression, long before she knew how true it could be.

She had also written the roller coaster story, which hadn't done anything at all. That one wasn't as fun to think about. Instead, J.R. wondered, who was the someone who had sent

Ms. Kline to her? More importantly, what did that someone think J.R. was struggling to say?

Then there was the bad that came with the good, according to her teacher. That didn't sound so great. J.R. thought through her stories. Ms. Kline had said she got a free pass with her first one, and it was true that J.R. couldn't think of anything bad that happened from walking home alone. With her second story, it was hard to argue with the fact that Ava had suffered from getting sick. Scoring that goal had been pretty amazing, although the look on the goalie's face reminded J.R. that not everyone felt the same way. Last, there was the phone. It was ironic that despite her parents' fears, nothing had gone wrong. Still, J.R. would have to be careful with whatever she wrote next. She would feel terrible if she made something really bad happen.

J.R. thought back to some of the things Ms. Kline had been clearer about, like "no shortcuts," although maybe she had been more emphatic than clear, and "focus on dialogue." Ms. Kline also recommended reading what she wrote out loud. J.R. studied her new cover. She loved Halloween and still wanted to celebrate with Violet. She started to write—or really to rewrite something like what she wished she could have responded with at lunch when Violet said she was co-ordinating costumes with Ava. For once, Ms. Kline's instructions made perfect sense: The conversation would definitely require putting herself out there and taking a risk.

HERE'S HOW I FEEL

"What should we be for Halloween this year?" Maya asked her best friend, Grace. "How about a carrot and a stick?"

That was kind of a joke. Their soccer coach had offered carrots (Popsicles) or sticks (extra laps) at their last practice of the spring season. By the time they started up again in the fall, it was back to business and laps.

"Maybe?" Grace mushed her cheeks and forehead into a skeptical face. "I was thinking we could invite Alice, and the carrot and stick only works for two people."

Maya would never admit it, but that was the point. Alice was new at school and had instantly befriended Grace. "Don't you think it would be okay to invite her but let her go in her own costume?"

J.R. stopped and read over the story so far. She could hear her own voice in Grace and Maya. Deep down, she wished she could be like parts of both characters, but it was hard: Maya trying to ask for what she wanted, and Grace able to be generous toward the new girl. The friends became fictional role models.

> "I guess," Grace said. "Or really, I don't
> think so. I think we should find something
> that's good for all three of us."
>
> Maya wanted to simply agree because she
> didn't like to argue. But suddenly her feelings
> tumbled out.

Just the thought of tumbling-out emotions made J.R. jealous of the girl on the page. It would be so nice to say what she wanted without worrying.

> "It's not okay," Maya said. "I mean, I know
> it's not that nice, but I don't really want Alice
> around. I get that she's new, and needs friends,
> and you're being friendly. Or maybe you really
> like her. But what about me?"
>
> Maya heard her voice get a little shrill. She
> didn't like it, but she couldn't help herself.
>
> "What about you?" Grace asked. Her voice
> was all challenge.
>
> "What about how I feel? What about how I
> feel left out by you and your new friend?"

J.R. wasn't sure it was quite the direct question Ms. Kline assigned, but when she backed up and read the last few paragraphs out loud, she could imagine herself talking that way. Almost. At least it definitely wasn't too preciously phrased to sound real. It was harder to answer Maya's question, though. She decided to write what she wished Grace would say, even though it felt like cheating, like maybe Maya hadn't made a persuasive enough argument to get the result she hoped for.

"Then I'm really sorry. I didn't realize. I didn't mean it. Forget about Alice," Grace concluded.

Chapter 17

WHEN SCHOOL ENDED THE NEXT day and Violet asked if she was ready to go to Taylor's, J.R. wasn't at all surprised.

"Ready," she answered, as if picking out costumes together had always been their plan. It did take some effort to act so nonchalant. Even if the change wasn't nearly as surprising as it would have been when sixth grade started, it was still a thrill to write a story and see what came next.

As they headed south toward the store, Tommy called out for them to wait. J.R. and Violet turned around and watched as he jogged the half block until he caught up. His manny didn't bother hustling and let the distance between them grow. "Where are you guys going?"

"Taylor's," Violet answered. "We're getting costumes for Curtis's party." The McBride family's annual Halloween party had become a tradition. The whole class got invited and could just fit in the McBrides' big apartment if they squeezed.

Curtis's mom went all out on decorations. The only bad thing was that this year Halloween fell on a Saturday, which meant the party conflicted with trick-or-treating. The good thing was that J.R. could stop worrying about whether Violet would have wanted to trick-or-treat with her or with Ava.

"Can I come?" Tommy asked, taking an exaggerated breath. Violet agreed before J.R. could object. "Cool," Tommy said. "I haven't even started planning."

J.R. could not say the same. She had spent hours looking for ideas online. A bright-tailed peacock looked awesome but impractical, and a lemon-lime pair that was more dresses than costumes would have been great, too. Coordinating costumes with Violet was too much to hope for, though. At least they were keeping their Taylor's tradition alive.

Inside the store, a huge sign that said TWEEN hung from the ceiling and directed them toward the back.

"'Tween' is just the worst word," Violet groaned. "Let's look over here." She nudged the group toward the full-fledged teen section, which had slightly bigger sizes and noticeably more provocative costumes. A French painter caught J.R.'s eye. It came with a blue-and-white-striped shirt, red beret, and fake black mustache. Taylor's had a huge art supply section, and a paintbrush and palette would complete the look.

"How about this?" Violet asked, holding up a bag for J.R.'s inspection. It had a picture of a maid on the outside. "Could be a good one for you," Violet teased while extracting the costume from the wrapping. The skirt was so short and the front of the top was so low that they practically met in the middle. As color spread across his cheeks, Tommy continued down the aisle to the boys' section. J.R. noticed that he still stayed close.

"Come on. Live a little!" Violet prodded. "You can tell your parents that you're Martha." J.R. started to say that this time, her parents weren't the problem. She would never wear the costume even if they'd let her. Besides, Martha was a twelve-year-old maid in much more conservative clothes—a 1929 mystery-solving maid, to be more specific—not a provocateur. J.R. and Violet both thought she was a pretty great main character when they read *The Gallery* the year before.

J.R. did start to question her instinct to go as an animal or citrus fruit, though, or even an amusing French artist. Maybe she wanted a costume that was a little more grown-up. Violet's suggestion offered inspiration.

J.R. scanned the racks until she found what she was looking for, a black sequined flapper costume with fringe at the bottom and a sparkly headband to pull across her forehead. It was perfect.

"Yes!" Violet said when J.R. held up her selection. The picture on the bag had a girl in fishnet stockings and heels with a long cigarette holder in her hand. J.R. didn't plan to add those extras, but the dress and hairpiece were included, and she could buy a black feather boa without spending a lot more. "I love it," Violet gushed. "You're going to look awesome!"

Hearing Violet's enthusiasm, Tommy came over to see what they found.

"It's for J.R." Violet pointed to the bag. He nodded approvingly. "What about you?"

"Nothing great," Tommy said, although he didn't sound disappointed by the unsuccessful search. "I've got a few ideas up my sleeve." Tommy winked, and the girls groaned.

"Maybe Houdini?" Violet asked. "I bet Margaret would let you borrow her bunny." The three of them laughed. Margaret had a pet white rabbit named Diamond that she talked about constantly. The idea of a rabbit hutch in a New York City apartment was not at all appealing.

"Not Houdini," Tommy called over his shoulder, heading toward the door. "Better. You'll see."

"Okay, then," Violet said after Tommy disappeared. "We'll see, indeed!"

It took Violet forever to find something that inspired her—long enough, even, that J.R. was ready to get going. After studying a cheerleader, a witch, and a hippie, she finally settled on Cleopatra, with a long white dress, black wig, and a gold arm cuff with a snake head on the end.

"Perfect!" J.R. said when Violet located her size.

"Perfect," Violet echoed dreamily.

The girls took their purchases to the front of the store, where

J.R. was not surprised this time to find extra money in her wallet. She paid for her costume and stuck it in her backpack.

"Oops," Violet said when it was her turn to check out. "I forgot to get eye makeup. Don't you want some, too?"

"My parents wouldn't like it. I'm not going to push my luck."

"Suit yourself." Violet smiled mischievously. "I'm definitely going to push mine!"

Chapter 18

"YOU LOOK GREAT!" J.R.'S MOM exclaimed when her daughter entered the living room on the Saturday night of Curtis's party. The black sequined dress and feather boa were definitely a departure from J.R.'s usual style. Her mother had bought her a pair of simple black slip-ons the weekend before, which was nice since J.R.'s only other shoes were sneakers. "Wait one second." Her mom called for a pause with her pointer finger before disappearing into her bedroom. After opening and closing drawers rather loudly, she eventually returned with a long strand of pearls. "Let's add these—but be careful with them. They were your grandmother's."

J.R. put on the necklace and took a look in the hallway mirror. The pearls were the perfect accessory. "Thanks," she said, and gave her mom a hug. It dawned on her mid-squeeze that she hadn't done that in a while.

"Ready to go?" her dad asked.

"You don't need to walk me anymore, remember?"

"But what if I want to?"

J.R. shook her head in defeat, but really she didn't mind. It would be nice to have company. The two of them headed for Curtis's party. Costumed kids were already out in full force, streaming out of the tall buildings and going door-to-door to get candy from the brownstones where residents set up shop on their stoops. J.R. and her dad stopped to check out the jack-o'-lanterns at June's. Alex had commissioned someone to carve the pumpkins, and they were always amazing. This time, one had a picture of Sal with her pail of blueberries walking up Blueberry Hill. *Blueberries for Sal* was one of J.R.'s favorite books when she was little, so she was especially excited about that one. Another, carved into an elongated pumpkin, looked like the cover of *The Crossover*. Josh was wearing high-tops and long shorts, and balancing a basketball on his finger. The third jack-o'-lantern was the most elaborate. It showed the mother from *The Runaway Bunny* up in the clouds blowing wind into her baby's ears, which looked like sails, as the little rabbit floated away. J.R.'s father complimented Alex on the year's selection before grabbing a Jolly Rancher for the walk.

At the intersection of Madison Avenue and 85th Street, they stopped to wait for the light. A mother and daughter stood at the corner passing out flyers that said LOST! in what looked like a kid's handwriting. "Three-year-old black-and-white mutt with a white streak down her nose and white-tipped tail. Answers to Raven. Beloved. Precious. Perfect. Please help bring her home!"

"Pretty flowery language," J.R.'s dad whispered. "Reminds me of something you would have written, except not about a dog, of course." J.R. shot down her dad's joke with a disapproving look. Her parents' refusal to get a puppy remained a sore spot.

"I'm sorry about Raven," J.R. said to the girl, who looked like she was about eight. Her eyes were red and swollen. "What happened?"

"I took her out in front of our building to go to the bathroom. Then there was a big bang, like two cars getting into an accident, and Raven just ran off. I wasn't," she mumbled, catching her breath like she was going to cry, "I wasn't holding on tightly enough to the leash."

"Well, these things happen," J.R.'s dad said consolingly. "Black with a white-tipped tail, right? We'll definitely keep an eye out."

The girl sniffled and J.R.'s heart broke.

Two blocks later, the Silvers parted ways outside Curtis's building. After she rode the elevator to the eighth floor, J.R. took off her jacket and tried to cram it onto the portable coatrack in the hallway. As she did, she saw a pink-and-purple polka-dotted bag tucked underneath. It was the one Violet always packed for sleepovers. Next to it lay another bag with "Aria" stitched in red script, and one next to that with Adelaide's name on the outside. J.R. started to think she should have skipped the party.

"Well, look at that!" Tommy said as he stepped off the

elevator. "Partners in crime?" Tommy opened his coat wide to reveal a striped suit and red tie that complemented his fedora. He looked like a 1920s mobster.

"I'm not a criminal," J.R. said. It came out with some residual crankiness from her sleepover bag suspicions, which she really didn't mean to direct at Tommy. She was glad to have someone to walk into the party with.

"Fair enough," he conceded. "Shall we?" Tommy opened the door and let J.R. through.

Inside the apartment, they poked their heads into the den, where Margaret was playing chess with Curtis's little brother. A pair of skeletons positioned on the couch looked like they were in the middle of their own match. Mrs. McBride had replaced all the family photos on the bookshelves just for the party. In one, Curtis's brother ate an ice-cream cone, but next to him Curtis was just a translucent ice-cream-eating outline. In another, Mr. McBride manned a barbecue dressed as a warlock. A fan blew onto a witch hanging from the ceiling and made Margaret's hair flutter. "So annoying," she muttered to no one in particular.

"Skip the chess lair?" Tommy asked.

"Definitely."

A crowd had gathered around a fortune-teller in the living room. She wore a green silk shirt with a purple head wrap and sat at a card table reading palms with great solemnity. J.R. joined the end of the line behind Violet to have her palm read. Tommy headed for the snacks.

"You look incredible!" Violet said. Unaccustomed to wearing a dress, J.R. tugged at the hemline. Violet hadn't been kidding about her plans for heavy eye makeup. Layers of black paint completed her Cleopatra outfit. She held up her phone, threw her other arm around J.R., and took a photo.

"Hi there!" Ava appeared dressed in black tights, a long-sleeved leotard, and a bat-shaped mask. Aria and Adelaide, eating little bags of gummy worms and dressed as mummies, came over, too. Apparently, everyone had given up on the zombie pop star idea.

"I like your outfit." Adelaide surprised J.R. with a compliment. She put down the candy to tuck in a piece of bandage that had come undone on her arm. "Are you a flap?"

"The word is flapper," said Ava.

Adelaide blanched.

"Thanks. I like your costume, too," J.R. jumped in, unexpectedly sympathetic in the face of Ava's correction.

"Can I try those?" Ava pointed to the pearls. J.R. froze, remembering her mom's warning to keep the necklace safe, even though she was pretty sure Ava would be careful. She slipped the strand over her head and passed it to Ava. "They're so pretty," she said as she gently put them on. J.R. thought for a second that Ava was going to ask to keep them, but then she realized that was ridiculous. In fact, Ava quickly lost interest in the necklace. As J.R. watched, her attention drifted toward Curtis, who was holding court in front of a bunch of boys. They had taken the Viking helmets they made in class and added a selection of capes, boots, and swords to create full-fledged warrior costumes. "Thanks for letting me try them." Ava slid off the necklace and put it back on J.R., kind of like a coronation. "I like your costume a lot."

Before J.R. had time to respond, Ava took Violet's hand and pulled her toward the face-painting table, even though there wasn't room for more makeup on Violet's face. That probably wasn't the point. The table was near the boys.

"What are you doing tonight?" Adelaide asked when Violet and Ava were out of earshot.

"Huh?" J.R. didn't get the question. "I'm here."

"I meant afterward," Adelaide said.

Now J.R. understood. She wished she had caught on sooner. "We're driving out to my grandparents' house later. My grandmother's birthday is tomorrow."

"Oh, that's why you couldn't come to Ava's sleepover," Adelaide needled.

This, J.R. suspected, was the bad that came with the good from her Halloween story. She didn't want to give Adelaide the satisfaction of the response she was clearly looking for. Instead, J.R. answered, "My grandmother's turning seventy-five, so it's a pretty big deal."

"That is a big deal. I got to FaceTime with my grandmother in Buenos Aires for her birthday last week, but I wish we could have been there to celebrate." Aria seemed to be going out of her way to change the subject.

To J.R.'s surprise, Adelaide didn't go in for the kill. She

didn't ask if the reason J.R. wasn't going to Ava's house was because she hadn't been invited. Rather than give Adelaide time to change her mind, J.R. claimed to be thirsty and headed for the drinks table. She could probably count on one hand the number of times her parents had willingly let her have soda, so at least the Coke would be a treat.

As she poured herself a cup, Tommy appeared and motioned to the crowd of Viking-clad boys. "Fine line between laughter and slaughter?" He looked to J.R. to acknowledge his quip. "Get it? The only difference in spelling is the *s*? It was kind of a play on words, since they're dressed as Vikings but look totally ridiculous?"

Normally J.R. would have been amused, but Adelaide had really gotten to her. *Nothing about this is funny*, she thought. Determined to be a good friend, she managed to muster a laugh.

Chapter 19

J.R. WAS THE ONLY KID at her grandmother's birthday party, so no one objected when she took her plate to the backyard and sat on a lounge chair with her schoolbag full of homework. Alone by the pool, which was covered until the summer, she scrolled through her phone and picked at the scrambled eggs and pineapple she had picked from the buffet. Lots of people had posted pictures from Curtis's party, and J.R. was happy to see herself tagged in a few. She zoomed in on one and admired the sequined headband that went with her dress. Combined with her short hair, she actually looked like a pretty authentic flapper.

It wasn't so great to see all the pictures from Ava's sleepover. From what she could tell, the girls had watched a movie and made ice-cream sundaes, and Aria may have fallen asleep in her mummy outfit, or at least J.R. thought it was Aria rather than Adelaide. Nine hours earlier, or around two in the morning, Violet had posted a picture of Ava and Louis, who looked really cute in his bumblebee dog costume. J.R. had been asleep for hours by then. Apparently, the girls weren't the only ones still awake, though—Matt Ghent commented right after.

Tired of looking at her classmates' pictures, J.R. wondered who else she could follow on Instagram, or maybe what else. Nic had an account that mostly chronicled sports teams and school plays. She looked up the Met and flipped through various pictures of Central Park. Then she searched for June's Books. There were a couple of pictures from an author's visit the week before, and a display of Halloween-themed books. Her parents had given up on making her stop by the store once she got her phone. Now she kind of missed it.

June's had posted a few pictures already that morning. One showed three men and a woman sitting at the middle table. They each had a book in front of them, as well as a box of coffee and a bunch of paper cups. J.R. recognized the man she had seen leaving the store a few weeks earlier with the sports books. Whoever created the post had added the hashtags #booksforlife and #coffeeonsunday. Something in the back of the photo caught J.R.'s eye. Standing behind the group, appearing to whisper, were Alex and Ms. Kline, or at least someone who looked a lot like her. The woman was facing away from the camera, but she had Ms. Kline's same low bun, impeccable posture, and all-black outfit. Plus, she was holding George. Only Ms. Kline, J.R. thought, could bond with that finicky cat. But Ms. Kline had told the class that she lived in

Brooklyn. What was she doing early on a weekend all the way uptown, and what was she whispering about with Alex?

J.R. opened her backpack, pulled out her *Gothamite* folder, and found her Halloween story, which definitely felt like it had mixed results in the wake of Curtis's party and Ava's sleepover. Ms. Kline had taken a few weeks to return her comments while also taking an agonizing break from giving out new *Gothamite* assignments. *Not exactly glowing,* J.R. thought as she reread her teacher's notes, although she appreciated her own jack-o'-lantern pun.

J.R.:

Pretty good. I could hear your voice say, "But what about me?" Can we both admit it sounded kind of whiny? Isn't there a better way for Maya to express herself?

Let's think about Grace here, too. Try putting yourself in her shoes. It would be tough to balance Maya's feelings with her own, and with Alice's feelings, too. Shouldn't we cut her some slack?

At this point in the semester, it's helpful to pause, and you may have noticed we've been focusing on other work, although of *course there are always opportunities to put what you've learned into practice. I think it would be good to go back through your assignments. What did I ask of you each time, not just with regard to literary devices, which are important for everyone to work on—but what else did the instructions say? Did you do it? Take a look and give it some thought.*

Shouldn't we cut her some slack? J.R. read again to herself. Ugh. J.R. felt like she was the one who deserved some slack. And then as soon as she thought it, she knew how it sounded: kind of whiny, too.

J.R. hadn't yet taken Ms. Kline's advice to go back through her assignments. With the adults chattering away inside and not much else to do, it was as good a time as any. She pulled out the stories she had collected in the folder and put them in order from first to last. She considered each one and could hear Ms. Kline giving snippets of her instructions—were these the instructions her comments were referring to?

There was the lonely looking girl on the first day of school, the one that started everything.

This is your chance to make the world about you, Ms. Kline had said.

Next came the girl pretending to be sick. *Break down the wall between the page and real life*, whatever that meant.

For the quick soccer story, it was *don't second-guess yourself.*

Then for the phone, *advocate for your protagonist.*

The Halloween story instructions were a little more serious: *Take a risk.* And now in her note, Ms. Kline was telling J.R. to be more open-minded. Just the fact that her teacher was compelled to give that advice didn't feel great.

J.R. took out the magazine she had picked for the current weekend's assignment. It was a picture of some still-leafy birch trees covered in snow. The covers Ms. Kline had displayed on Friday had been unusual: There were no people in any of them. She told the class to think about symbolism, which they had talked a lot about when they read *El Deafo.* The author made her characters into bunnies with big ears, which Ms. Kline said was poignant since the author herself was deaf and aware as a kid that her ears didn't work like most people's. To give an example of symbolism in the *Gothamite* covers, Ms. Kline had held up one from 1987 with a man in a suit outside the New York Stock Exchange walking a fox instead of a dog. Foxes symbolized greed, she said, which J.R. had never heard before.

There was one cover that had looked particularly intriguing, but she had been too slow to scoop it up. It showed a map of the United States with three arcs: a complete Gateway Arch in the middle of the country over St. Louis, Missouri; half of the Golden Gate Bridge, but rather than spanning the San Francisco Bay, it left the city and stretched east until it met up with the Arch in St. Louis; and then half of the Brooklyn

Bridge, which picked up where the Golden Gate left off and connected back to New York City. J.R. hadn't known how to interpret the cover, but she had noted the date—October 1989—and planned to find out what was going on in the news. Unfortunately, she couldn't remember the precise day, but it was sometime close to Halloween, as best she could recall.

J.R. picked up her phone to try to figure out what was happening around that time—was there an actual event that the artist was commenting on? Before she crafted her search, she had another idea unrelated to the assignment. There was an important cover that J.R. hadn't thought much about, the one that Ms. Kline had pasted to the front of her folder. The joyful ballerina never made much sense, at least as far as it related specifically to her.

J.R. searched *"Gothamite* Ballerina Cover" on her phone and scrolled through the results. There were girls in red leotards in what looked like a ballet class, a ballerina applying makeup in front of a well-lit mirror, and a few others that weren't right. Then her cover appeared. J.R. clicked on the image, which brought up the title: "Leap of Faith in Herself."

Chapter 20

AFTER A PAINFULLY OFF-TUNE RENDITION of "Happy Birthday" and a lot of cleaning up, the Silvers said goodbye to J.R.'s grandmother and drove back to Manhattan. They had parked their car and were nearly home when they ran into Alex, who was waiting to cross the street outside June's.

"Hi!" J.R. said as soon as she saw him. Her greeting came out with an unintended level of enthusiasm, but their meeting felt quite lucky. If Ms. Kline insisted on being opaque with her answers, maybe Alex would be more forthcoming. All these strange connections couldn't be coincidences. "I think I need a book," she said to her parents. "Can I go with Alex to June's?"

"Actually, Maria's holding down the fort, and I'm on my way to the Met."

"What are you going to see? The tapestry show is magnificent, if you haven't been." J.R.'s mom gave her daughter a pointed look as she spoke. After Violet had rejected her invitation, J.R. hadn't brought herself to walk through the exhibition. Nor had she told her mom why.

"I don't have anything specific in mind. Just felt like taking a look around."

"Well, I know an excellent tour guide."

"Dad!" J.R. exclaimed. Her father could be so embarrassing. "But I do feel like going to the museum. Is it okay if I join you?"

"Absolutely." Alex had a slightly amused look on his face.

"Just don't stay out too long," her dad added. "You have that French test tomorrow."

J.R.'s mom fished out their family membership card from her wallet. "Put that somewhere safe, will you?"

"Parents," J.R. groaned, then slipped the card into her back pocket, which probably wasn't the safest place.

Alex and J.R. headed west to Fifth Avenue and then south along the west side of the street, outside the wall bordering Central Park. The sidewalk was full of bumps, and a little girl on a yellow bike almost toppled over right in front of them before her mom grabbed the handlebars. A double-decker bus drove by, and some tourists waved from the seats on top. Outside the circling facade of the Guggenheim, a street vendor sold the first roasted chestnuts J.R. had seen for the season. The sweet, smoky scent wafted across the street. Every year, her dad bought them a bag to eat, but the taste was always disappointingly bland and the texture way too mealy. The chestnuts never lived up to their olfactory potential.

"What do you want to see?" Alex asked when they reached the museum. J.R. followed him through the side door toward the members' desk. It wasn't as nice as going up the front stairs and into the main lobby, but there was never a line. J.R. took Alex's approach as a sign that he knew his way around.

"Not sure. I do have a French test tomorrow and I haven't started studying, so I probably shouldn't stay too long."

"How about we each pick one thing, and that'll be it? You first. Show me what you've got."

"Follow me," she said, leading them to the back of the lobby and up a flight of stairs, where they emerged in the Oceanic art section. J.R. took them through two rooms of glass-enclosed sculptures until they got to a gallery full of art from New Guinea. Hanging from the ceiling was the enormous roof of a ceremonial house made from a jumble of painted and roughly rectangular wooden slabs. J.R. guessed that the footprint was bigger than their entire apartment building.

"The Kwoma Ceiling. Great pick," Alex said admiringly.

J.R. felt a tinge of disappointment. She should have taken him to something more obscure, even if the ceiling was truly incredible. They walked closer and stood just outside the railing that enclosed a wooden crocodile and some other carvings beneath the roof. "That one's my favorite." J.R. pointed upward. "The panel that looks like a man with a heart-shaped mouth."

"Looks more like a woman to me."

J.R. figured he was joking. She wasn't sure the image was

even meant to be a human face, although it did look like one. J.R. started to zone out.

"What's up?" Alex asked.

"Just thinking. Violet would really like this."

Alex didn't say anything, and J.R. weighed how best to continue. She actually wanted to talk, although it was hard to put her worries into words. "I'm not sure she wants—" She started again. "Violet and I used to be really good friends. We hung out all the time. But now she hangs out with Ava, and not just her but these two other girls in my class."

"Who you don't like?"

"Well, I'm not sure about them." J.R. knew the other kids weren't really the problem. The problem was sharing Violet. Not only that, but what if J.R. did what Alex and Ms. Kline asked and gave them all a try? What if they didn't try her back?

"Have you talked to her about it? That seems like the first step."

His matter-of-fact tone rubbed J.R. wrong. "Easy for you to say."

"It's true. She's not my friend, she's yours. But it sounds like she's a good one. So if she was my friend, I'd fight for her." J.R. silently absorbed his advice. "Okay, my turn to pick." They climbed one flight of stairs into a sea of European paintings. Alex clearly knew where he was going and navigated to the side of a room full of nineteenth-century pictures by the French painter Camille Corot. When he sat down on the puffy leather bench in the middle of the gallery, J.R. planted herself beside him.

"Did you have a specific painting in mind?" she asked. The room wasn't exactly the museum's most exciting.

"*Sibylle.*" Alex pointed to the portrait of a woman on the wall. She had dark black hair and held a red rose in her left hand in front of her chest. Her other hand lay on her lap. J.R. was puzzled by the choice. The woman sat in front of a drab gray background with a look on her face that was somewhere between impassive and sad. "See the way she's holding that flower?" Alex asked. "Looks strange, doesn't it?" It was true. The woman's hand curled inward at an odd angle. "That's because when Corot first painted the picture, she was playing a cello. The portrait makes sense if you imagine her holding its neck."

Now that Alex said it, it was easy to picture Sibylle with a cello, her fingers on the strings. "But what about her right hand? Was she holding a bow?"

"Not sure. Maybe she was, and then Corot moved it to her lap instead."

"How do you know all that?"

"X-rays. Or really, I read about X-rays they used to see the paint underneath."

"That's pretty cool." J.R. was impressed. She was already looking forward to sharing news about the hidden cello on Monday. The old Violet would have been up for a trip to the museum to check it out. Hopefully, the new Violet would be as excited.

"Seemed like a boring pick at first, didn't it? But you need to look closely. Otherwise, you can't always see what's really going on, especially with people."

J.R. had been distracted by Sibylle, but Alex's words snapped her back to why she had wanted to talk to him in the first place. She channeled Claudia from the *Mixed-Up Files*. When Jamie tries to convince his sister that they should go home, Claudia doesn't agree. She says that if they go back already, nothing will be different. She needs to solve the mystery behind Angel, the statue, first. Then she will be a heroine, and then she'll be different for sure.

J.R. didn't aspire to that kind of change, but the afternoon set her on her own sort of mission, and she was determined not to go home without answers. She looked around and confirmed they were alone. "Can I ask you a question?"

"Shoot," Alex said.

"How do you know Kate Kline?"

The corners of his mouth quivered upward. "She's an old friend, although I didn't really get to know her well until more recently."

"She's my teacher, you know?" Alex nodded. "Did you meet at a reunion?"

"That's right, we did."

"Was it the same reunion when you met the man who drew that *Gothamite* cover for your wedding?" J.R. knew the pieces were coming together.

"Same group of people, different reunion. Harry and I met

earlier. My wife had already passed away by the time I met Kate. June would have liked her, though."

J.R. stopped for a second. Alex sounded serious but not sad. She was pretty sure she could continue. "What kind of reunion was it?"

"Good question. It was a reunion of students who knew the same teacher, a woman named Eleanor Mendell."

J.R. mentally checked that box. "Ms. Kline's told us about her, and I found her obituary." Taking Ms. Kline's Halloween assignment to heart, J.R. decided to ask some direct questions. "Was Ms. Mendell your sixth-grade teacher?"

"She was." Two women entered the gallery. Alex waited to be sure they were absorbed in their own conversation before he continued. "When Eleanor Mendell found me, I was the shyest kid in my class. I barely talked. But I always loved books, and she drew out my voice. First, she gave me the confidence to talk about them in class, and then I went from there."

"Did Ms. Mendell have her *Gothamite* collection back then?"

Alex frowned. "How old do you think I am? She had those magazines forever. A lot of kids used them before me!"

"Okay, sorry." J.R. held up her hands in surrender. "So when Ms. Mendell gave you *Gothamite* assignments, did something special happen?"

"Indeed it did." Now Alex really smiled.

"Same for your wife, and for Ms. Kline? And maybe for Harry, too?"

"You got it!" Alex held up his hand for a high five. In her excitement, J.R. didn't feel self-conscious about obliging. Instead, she felt like they were entirely in sync and decided to keep going.

"Remember that time you came to my apartment when I was getting on the phone?" Alex nodded. "Were you talking to Ms. Kline?" Another nod. "And did you come because you knew I was about to tell Violet what was going on and you wanted to stop me?"

"Close," Alex said with a final dip of his chin. "Kate was pretty sure, and she asked me to go check." J.R.'s expression made clear she was confused. "You see, Kate and I were Eleanor's students, but Kate went on to become a teacher. And Kate's the teacher who inherited Eleanor's magazine collection. That act rekindled, shall we say, some of the magazines' magic for her. She has a special way of intuiting things now, of knowing what's really going on with her students. It's a gift that is reserved for the teachers who steward the collection."

"I knew those magazines were magic!" J.R. exclaimed.

"Hold on." Alex actually held up his palm to stop her, which was good because J.R. would have kept babbling. "The magazines aren't magic, or at least not exactly. The magazines can tap a certain magic *in you*. But *you* have to work for it." With that nugget of wisdom, Alex stood up to leave. It felt like the kind of thing Ms. Kline would do, to shut down the conversation just as it got interesting. "Are you coming?" he asked. "I thought you had a French test to study for."

J.R. took one more look at Sibylle. "Are we really leaving? I have more questions."

"You're so close, J.R. I know you'll get there." Alex started to walk off. "I may take a few more minutes to look around, so you go home and study. We'll talk more later. I'm sure Kate told you that there are consequences, intentional or not, to your stories. No more sick classmates, right?" J.R. wondered exactly how Alex knew about that, but she didn't dare to ask. Ms. Kline had probably spilled the beans. "Try doing something selfless," he said. "It'll feel good."

Alex didn't say goodbye. Instead, he headed out of the gallery. J.R. stayed where she was and tried to understand what he meant. The last thing she wanted to do was study. Luckily, she had a solution to that problem as soon as she got back to her magazine cover. It was convenient that snow was often seen as magical—a symbol of sorts—and that a blanket of snow was so much fun. Maybe, she thought, the French test could wait.

Chapter 21

"IT'S GOOD TO SEE EVERYONE again," Ms. Kline said on Tuesday morning. "I hope you enjoyed the unexpected long weekend."

"That was awesome, right?" Tommy smiled so broadly that light actually flashed off his braces.

Getting a snow day on Monday was definitely awesome, and J.R. hoped Ms. Kline would appreciate how well she had executed the assignment. Now, sitting in class, waiting to turn in her blizzard story, she could feel her chest puff out slightly. It was so tempting to answer Tommy by alluding to her role in their day off from school. J.R. had to pinch her palm to make herself stop.

"I need a few minutes to get set up," said Ms. Kline while she went to her filing cabinet to take out some magazines. "In the meantime, please work on your longship drawings. I'd like to try to get those up on the walls this week."

While Ms. Kline took longer than usual to make her

selections, the class got out colored pencils to continue the Viking longship drawings they were working on, complete with labels for each part of their boats. Sketching had never been one of J.R.'s talents, and her ship looked shorter and fatter than she had intended, with a red-and-white-striped sail that wasn't quite centered on the mast. Carlos's drawing was pretty amazing—it was as good as any of the pictures Ms. Kline had projected on the whiteboard when talking to them about the ships. When the teacher was finally organized and caught sight of his work, she came over to admire the picture more closely.

"Now, that is remarkable!" she said. "I didn't know we had such a gifted illustrator in our midst. When I hang these up, yours is going front and center."

Carlos looked a little embarrassed and a little pleased. Margaret looked miffed. Before she had time to call Ms. Kline's attention to her picture, the teacher left to finish laying out another round of magazines along the windowsills.

"For your homework tonight, I would like you to think about character," Ms. Kline said. "I know we dipped into this topic with the first assignment, but it's time to circle back because character development is such an important part of storytelling. Think of it as our own little narrative arc." No one laughed at Ms. Kline's attempt at writing humor. "So please pick a single character to focus on from the cover you choose, someone entirely unlike yourself. Then practice seeing the world through their eyes. How do they perceive the situation you've put them in? How do the facts you throw at them make them feel? And here's an important part: I want your character to do something nice for someone else, something generous of spirit." That sounded a lot like the selflessness Alex had mentioned, J.R. thought. Ms. Kline cleared her throat. "No stories about the weather, please."

"Who would write about the weather?" Tommy asked.

"No idea," J.R. answered as casually as she could.

Two minutes later, the magazines were ready, as was J.R. She needed to find another cover that would help repair her relationship with Violet. It couldn't be a coincidence that Alex and Ms. Kline had both said to do something nice. Was J.R. not a good friend? She definitely thought she was, but now she was worried and especially anxious to get started.

As her classmates made their choices, Tommy found J.R. to show her a cover. The picture looked over the shoulder of a man in a dimly lit theater. He was doing a crossword puzzle while waiting for the movie to start. A couple walked down the aisle with a huge bucket of popcorn, searching for seats. The title of the movie—*The Boxer*—was projected on the screen.

"I remember when my parents got this issue in the mail," Tommy said. "You know how they show the title the artist gives the cover in the table of contents?" J.R. gave Tommy an "of course I know" look. "This one's called 'Ere I saw Ali.' Isn't that good?"

It was, in fact, the perfect title, and perfect for Tommy. J.R.

knew from doing the crossword puzzle with her dad that "Ali" and "ere"—the famous boxer and the old-fashioned word for "before"—were both common answers, and it sounded a lot like the palindrome "Able was I ere I saw Elba," although it didn't actually work backward. "Wow," she said, making her own palindrome joke. "I should pick something, too."

"I'll help," Tommy offered. From the closest window, he took a cover with a baby crawling on top of a pile of Persian carpets. His parents, seemingly immersed in buying a rug, weren't paying attention at all. J.R. shook her head.

Tommy picked up another one with three men in suits, sunglasses, and earpieces guarding a dog that was burying a bone on the White House lawn. Pink cherry trees flowered in the background. It was funny, but it had nothing to do with her and Violet.

"I saw one over there that you might like," Tommy said, pointing to the whiteboard. "It had a woman dressed like a suffragette sitting behind a desk in a really modern office." J.R. went to find it, but someone else got there first.

Then a cover caught her eye. J.R. bent down for a closer look. The dog in the picture had shaggy black fur with a white stripe down its nose and a white-tipped tail. She looked a lot like the missing dog on the flyers plastered around J.R.'s neighborhood. In the drawing, she was sitting alone by the edge of Conservatory Water, the shallow pond on the eastern edge of Central Park. Two summers ago, Nina had taken J.R. with Violet and her brothers to sail little toy boats in the water. From the yellow light in the drawing, it looked like early morning, which was probably why there was no one around. The leg and chest of a lone jogger peeked into the top left of the picture, and a squirrel climbed up a tree in the foreground.

"Raven," J.R. whispered, remembering the name of the sad little girl's dog. J.R. straightened up and pressed the cover to her chest. Most of her classmates were back at their desks already.

"That's a smart choice," Ms. Kline said, appearing by J.R.'s side. The teeniest, tiniest smile emanated from her lips. J.R. was sure she could do something nice with the cover and already felt good about her pick.

When school let out that afternoon, the street was slushy. Most of the snow had melted and left gray puddles behind. The grossest ones had a layer of shiny oil on top. J.R. went straight to her apartment and dug out last year's snow pants, which were definitely too short. Then she retrieved her notebook, stuffed her headband in her pocket, and grabbed a handful of pretzels on her way back out the door, along with the spare MetroCard her mom kept in an envelope on the fridge. She was on a mission.

Twenty minutes later, J.R. was in Central Park at the edge of Conservatory Water, which wasn't very watery since it had already been drained for the winter. Walking home alone from school was one thing, but her parents definitely had not given her permission to wander this far on her own. She had to be quick, but for some reason being there felt key to her inspiration. Snow in the park always melted slower than it did on the streets, and there were still a few patches left on the grass. J.R. found a spot on the slope south of the pond and planted herself on the ground. Her pants kept her bottom dry but not warm, which was an extra incentive to hurry. She put on her headband and took the cover from her backpack. Sitting in the park, it was easy to see the world from Raven's perspective.

ADVENTURE OF THE LOST AND FOUND

Early morning is the best time, before kids descend on the playgrounds and the vendors roll out their carts. The hot dogs smell amazing, but I need to lie low when people are around. Dogs without humans arouse suspicion. I hadn't meant to leave Sophie, but I got scared, and I ran without thinking. Once I tasted freedom, it was hard to go back.

Living in the park has been quite an adventure. I really owe Sam the Squirrel, who has been so kind as to share his acorns even though they're not really my thing. All that work to crack the shell, and then there's just a dry nut inside. Luckily, Sam's given me tips on scavenging—the trash cans by the ice rink and

around the Great Lawn are full of treasures.
I do miss the ease of a pre-poured bowl of dog
food sometimes.

The novelty of camping has started to wear
off now that it's getting chilly. Sam's taught
me a lot about making a good home outdoors,
but I miss my bed, and my Sophie. I'm sure
she's worried. And I bet she misses my kisses in
the morning.

J.R. thought about some of Ms. Kline's earlier lessons,
about being sure to set the scene and using details to make
the story feel real. She tried to apply what she had learned.

Before I go home, though, I want one last
sunrise at the boat pond as the light starts to
sparkle on the water, so I made sure to get up
early today. Before long, I see the first morning
jogger. Normally, I try to stay away when people
show up, but I can tell he's my guy, and I head
straight for him. Hopefully, he's smart enough
to get me back to my apartment—I mean, he
just has to read my collar. If all goes well, I'll
have breakfast with Sophie before she leaves for
school.

"Woof, woof." In dog that means "Over here!
Can you help me?"

The man kneels down when I run to him.
Humans do that when they want to give you a
rub. "Are you lost, boy?"

I hold up my chin for a scratch, although
it puts my nose a little too close to his sweat.
I also want to tell him I'm a girl, but that's
beside the point. He's checking my collar and
pulling out a phone. Despite the sweaty smell, I
like this guy: a man of action! I can tell he'll get
me home.

J.R. knew she was done when she wrote the final period. She didn't even need to reread her work. J.R. waved her pencil around in three tight circles. "Bibbidi-Bobbidi-Boo!" she said with full fairy godmother gusto. It felt pretty good to work her magic. She packed up and headed out of the park to find a bus going toward home. Too amped up to be alone when she got there, J.R. stopped by June's. A family was leaving with a bag full of books, and Maria was helping an elderly woman in the biography section. Alex stood behind the cash register but didn't look up.

"Hi," J.R. said as she headed toward him. Alex quickly shuffled the papers he was holding. "Everything okay?"

"Of course," he said, not very reassuringly. "Just making my way through some mail. I'll be back in a second." Alex opened a drawer and stuck the papers inside. Then he disappeared into his office.

J.R. knew she shouldn't do it, but she was overwhelmed by the temptation to open the drawer. She had felt nervous, but not particularly guilty, about snooping through Ms. Kline's file cabinet, but this time she really knew it was wrong. Even so, J.R. glanced around to make sure Maria was fully occupied and pulled gently on the handle. The letter at the top of a pile bore the name Riley, Riddle & Mott, LLP, which sounded kind of familiar. The paper looked quite crinkled, like it had been around for a while and read a lot. J.R. picked it up.

Dear Mr. Richardson,

We are sorry to inform you that June's Books' current lease, which expires March 31, will not be renewed. We regret this development, but the new owner's plans for the building are not compatible with the current use of the space. Please ensure the store is empty and broom-clean by that date. Should you have any questions, you may contact me at the number below.

Sincerely,
Mary Ellen Marcus
Attorney-at-Law

J.R. stuffed the letter into the envelope but didn't get it back inside the drawer before Alex reemerged. "What are you doing?"

"I'm sorry," J.R. stammered. "I just—"

"You invaded my privacy." Alex sounded genuinely annoyed. Then he looked nervously at Maria and lowered his voice. "I hate that Maria is worried about this, but I'll work things out."

"Of course you will! Ms. Kline has the magazines," J.R. whispered with a knowing look.

"That's not how this works." Alex shook his head regretfully. "It's not so easy."

"But what are you going to do? June's can't close!" J.R. couldn't tell if he was resigned to defeat or ready for a fight.

"I don't know yet, but I don't want you to worry, either. And I don't want you to try anything silly. No magazine wishes about June's, all right?"

"Okay," J.R. said, to get Alex to stop.

"Promise?"

"Promise."

But of course J.R. worried. If Alex didn't have a solution, J.R. had to find one.

Chapter 22

ON THE WAY TO SCHOOL the next morning, J.R. passed the mother and daughter who had been looking for their dog. They were removing a sign taped to the coffee shop window around the corner from the Silvers' apartment. Raven stood next to them, wagging her tail. The mother held tightly to the leash while the girl rubbed the dog's back so vigorously that it was hard to imagine she actually liked it.

J.R.'s curiosity got the better of her. "Where did you find her?" she asked.

"A man who was running in the park said she just came up to him this morning. He recognized her from the signs," the girl said.

"And from the collar," the mom added wearily. "He brought her to our building. Poor guy was totally stressed because it made him late to work and he had some big meeting." J.R. shivered. That was the bad thing that came from the good, she supposed. Hopefully, he wasn't too late.

The girl kept talking a mile a minute. "When I got up for breakfast, Raven was waiting for me in the kitchen! It was the best breakfast I've ever had, weekday or weekend. Weekdays are worse since I have to rush to school, and weekends my dad usually makes pancakes. I'm going to make the man a present, or maybe I'll buy something. My mom got his address so we can send it."

"I'm glad," J.R. said, struggling to keep up with all the information. "I'm really, really glad." J.R. gave Raven a scratch behind her ears. It was a pretty good way to start the morning.

Two blocks later, J.R. had to wait for the light to cross the street. Jim sat up ahead in his usual spot. Although the sidewalk was now bare, the glow she had been enjoying faded when she realized that the snowstorm probably hadn't been such a thrill for everyone. When she reached his bench, she stopped.

"Hi," she said. "Sorry about all this snow."

"No need to apologize. Winter came early this year. Sometimes it happens." Jim had a book on his lap and a steaming cup of coffee on the bench beside him.

"What are you reading?" she asked.

"It's a biography of Robert Frost. You know him?"

"Of course I do." J.R. thought about one of his most famous poems, "Stopping by Woods on a Snowy Evening." She wondered if Jim had that poem in mind when he checked out the book.

"Frost grew up in the same town as me. A place called Lawrence, Massachusetts."

"I know where that is!"

"You do?"

"Right next to Haverhill." J.R. had once looked at a map after visiting the Haverhill Room to see where the house had been. Lawrence, which admittedly was also her grandfather's name, was one town over.

"Exactly right. Go figure." Jim smiled.

J.R. hesitated for a second, then offered her hand. "I'm J.R. It's nice to officially meet you."

J.R.'s first class was French, which was never very nice. Madame Moulin was a good teacher, but J.R. didn't have anyone to talk to. Violet and Tommy took Spanish like most of the kids in her grade, including Ava, of course. It seemed like there was never a time when she and Violet weren't together. Aria was already fluent in Spanish, so she was in J.R.'s French class, for better or worse.

"Find a partner," Madame Moulin said after the group trickled in. The whole class looked at her, puzzled. Madame Moulin never spoke English, not even when it was obvious that they had no idea what she was saying. "I have a terrible headache today," she explained. "Let's make this easy."

The teacher went on to divide the class into pairs. Each pair could use a laptop to research a food from a French-speaking country. They could even do their research in English. Everyone, she conceded, was getting a bit of a free pass. During their next class, they would give a presentation about what they found. Bonus points if they brought in the food to share. It all seemed pretty simple, except for J.R.'s partner. She got matched with Aria.

The two girls looked at each other before Aria nicely made the first move to switch seats so they could work together. She also opened up their laptop. "Any ideas?"

"Rien," J.R. said.

"Okay, then." Aria rolled her eyes with her words.

J.R. had meant it as a joke and realized she had probably sounded kind of rude. In an attempt to make quick amends, she offered a suggestion. "Maybe chocolate croissants?" After all, who didn't like chocolate croissants?

"We're doing croissants already!" Nathalie called out. She had a gross habit of popping her retainer in and out of her mouth after she spoke.

"All yours," Aria answered. "Too bad," she said to J.R. "Everyone likes chocolate croissants. Any other ideas?"

J.R. wanted to suggest something from the Francophone Caribbean, but she didn't know what. As she tried to come up with another suggestion, Aria beat her to it.

"How about poutine?" she asked.

"What's that?"

"Gravy-covered French fries that they eat in the French-speaking part of Canada. I had them last year when we went on vacation to Montreal, and they were amazing. My mom has

189

a friend with a restaurant in Brooklyn that makes them, so I bet we could even bring some in to try."

"I like any type of French fry, so I think that sounds perfect!"

In agreement about their savory solution, the girls turned back to the laptop and pulled up photos of poutines piled high in ceramic dishes. J.R. couldn't tell if they looked good or gross.

"But wait," J.R. said in a fake French accent. "You mentioned gravy, but here eet zays cheese curd also." She pointed to the white cottage-cheese-like substance on top of the fries.

"Zut alors! You are right." Aria exaggerated her accent even more than J.R. "I forgot. Zay are covered in zee cheese, and I promise zay are magnifique!" Aria blew a chef's kiss to compliment the dish.

The girls laughed and continued their research, downloading photos and recording a few facts, like that poutine was invented in rural Quebec in the 1950s, and that its exact origin was unknown and fiercely disputed.

"Have you ever been to Albertine?" Aria asked after a while.

"No," J.R. said reluctantly. "I've never left the country. I don't even have a passport."

"You don't need a passport! Albertine is in New York. It's a bookstore inside the French Embassy on Fifth Avenue, and it's got the most amazing ceiling. I mean, Ms. Kline's stars are cool, but Albertine's ceiling is painted in this incredible blue with constellations and planets on top of that in gold. You should check it out sometime."

"That does sound cool," J.R. answered. She was also interested to hear that Aria appreciated Ms. Kline's ceiling.

"You're pretty into writing, right? I remember the poem you published in *Nic Notes* last year." J.R. didn't realize Aria would have paid attention to the school's literary magazine or the fact that J.R.'s poem had been chosen for the first page. She wasn't exactly sure what to say but confirmed she did like to write. "There's a writing camp at the embassy for a week at the beginning of the summer, and my mom really wants me to go. It might be boring, but I'd rather do it with a friend." Aria's voice rose slightly in suggestion, and J.R. was pretty sure she had just received an invitation to go to camp with Aria.

"Writing in French, you mean? Aren't embassies for politics?"

"It's writing in French, and it's some sort of cultural part of the embassy, I think. Probably the main part is in Washington. But they show French movies in Central Park during the summer, and stuff like that. You know how zee French love zeir arts," Aria concluded, going back into her Frenchwoman-speaking-English voice.

"That does sound fun, but I think my parents are sending me to Wachusett," J.R. said, even though she wasn't sure why. Aria's question had caught her off guard. Plus, her parents definitely had not agreed to let her go to sleepaway camp, and she hadn't even raised the subject again recently.

"Oh, right," Aria said. "I should have realized." For a second, she looked like she was going to say something else, but then she dove back into the assignment, finding them more good facts about poutine and ramping up her fake French accent even more.

The rest of the period flew by. Aria was a lot more fun when Adelaide and Ava weren't around. Or maybe she was more fun, J.R. realized, when given a chance.

Chapter 23

IT TOOK MS. KLINE SEEMINGLY forever to return comments on J.R.'s dog story. By the time she finally handed back the assignments, J.R. was itching for feedback.

> J.R.:
>
> This is exactly what we are trying to accomplish: You did something generous. In addition, you really became the dog and brought her off the page. Sometimes it's easier to do that with a character that's nothing like yourself—a dog, in this instance. Next time, keep reaching deep but with a protagonist that's closer to your heart. Where the dog might say "woof," your human might say...?

J.R. groaned. Might say what?

"This is ridiculous." Tommy appeared beside J.R. in the courtyard after dismissal and pulled his Islanders hat over his ears. "I'm going home." He exhaled forcefully so his breath made a cloud.

J.R. and Tommy both had soccer practice right after school on Thursdays, although they were in the last week of the fall season. That was good because it was getting cold, and since the clocks had changed, it was also getting dark. By the time practice ended, anyone unlucky enough to have sent their ball far from the field by accident was guaranteed to have to search for it for a while. Tommy solved the problem by bringing a flashlight. Lately, J.R. noticed, he had started to wait for her after school so they could walk to the fields together. She supposed she was better company than his manny, who rarely took off his headphones. At least J.R. talked. She looked around the courtyard outside Nic to where Violet was standing with Ava and Matt while Curtis regaled them with a story. Both girls were laughing, and Matt was watching blankly. "I'm too cold to hang around," said Tommy, who quickly sized up the foursome. "Let's get going."

J.R. and Tommy set out toward Central Park. "He's kind of dead weight, no?" J.R. asked, pointing her thumb toward the babysitter trailing behind them.

Tommy shrugged, then reached into the bag of salt and vinegar chips he had extracted from his backpack. His fingers were stained blue from art class, where they had started painting a mural for the backdrop of their sea shanty show, which was scheduled for just before winter break. "My parents won't let me go to practice alone until the spring," he said. "Want some?" J.R. refused the chips. "Too unhealthful?" Tommy exaggerated the "ful," and J.R. laughed. To show her appreciation for his linguistic reference, J.R. held out her hand, palm up, to solicit some chips. The day's assembly speaker had talked about good nutrition and said that eating a whole bag of Doritos in one sitting was unhealthful—bad for your body. The nutritionist also noted that eating all those chips was not unhealthy, like most people would have said, since there was no such thing as a sickly bag of chips. "Will you still be my friend even though I've been using the wrong word to describe my snacks?"

"You're forgiven," J.R. said consolingly. "If I can have a few more chips."

Tommy handed over the bag. With his own mouth full, he began to hum the latest sea shanty they had learned in music. There were now six songs in their repertoire.

"I don't get that one," J.R. said before she sang the first line. "Oh Shenandoah, I long to see you. Aa-way you rolling river." She reached for another chip. "I mean, I thought sea shanties were about the sea, but that's about a river."

"Dunno," said Tommy. "But I like it. Kind of melancholy, though."

"Are you feeling melancholy?" J.R. teased.

Now Tommy looked serious. "Kind of."

"How come?" J.R. hadn't realized that Tommy was actually in a serious mood.

Tommy took back the bag and ate a few chips before he answered. "Something's up with my cousin, Max. He's a year older than me and lives on Long Island." J.R. couldn't help but chuckle. "What? I'm just telling you who he is."

"I know! I mean, I feel like I know Max from all the pictures you post and stories you tell!"

Tommy scowled. "Anyway, our birthdays are on the same day, and we always plan our parties a week apart so we can go to each other's. My party was on Saturday," Tommy explained. A worried look crossed his face. "Sorry I didn't invite you. It was just boys at Dave & Buster's."

"That's okay," J.R. assured him. "I'm not really into arcade games, anyway."

Tommy readily continued. "So when my mom called my aunt to give her the date, my aunt said that Max was having his party on Saturday, too. I guess he hadn't told me because he only invited his friends from his hockey team."

"Your cousin kind of sounds like a jerk."

"He's totally not a jerk," Tommy said emphatically. "That's the point. I can't believe he didn't invite me."

"I bet there was just some mix-up. You should ask him." J.R. didn't think there was a mix-up, but it was the best she could do.

"I did ask," Tommy said.

"Huh?"

"I did ask."

"You did?"

"I didn't want to, but my mom made me call him so I would stop moping."

"But what did you say to him?" J.R. really couldn't believe Tommy had called.

"I just told him how I felt."

"Well, what did you actually say?" J.R. wanted to know the exact words. She simply could not imagine how the conversation had unfolded.

"I asked why he hadn't invited me to his party."

"Just like that?"

"Just like that."

"And what did he say?"

"He said he was only having his hockey friends."

"But the question was *why* it was only for his hockey friends." J.R. heard the edge in her voice and wished she could take it back. She had to give Tommy credit for pursuing the conversation in the first place.

"I know," said Tommy. He looked a little irritated. "So I asked him why he couldn't have invited me, too. I mean, it wasn't like they were actually going to play hockey at the party. And if they wanted to talk about hockey, I could do that. I'm an Islanders fan."

"We know," J.R. said, eyeing his hockey jersey that had replaced his Mets gear. "So what did Max say?"

"He said he wanted to be with his hockey friends, and he was sorry if he hurt my feelings. He said he didn't mean to and he asked if my mom could bring me to his house next weekend."

"So are you going?"

"Yeah," said Tommy.

"And that's okay with you?" J.R. knew Tommy was going to say yes, but she couldn't understand it.

"I guess. I mean, I get it." Tommy sounded more like he was still talking himself into Max's explanation. "He's got a different group of friends that I'm not really part of, but that doesn't mean we're not still friends. It's just different. You know how that is."

"What do you mean?"

"I mean with Violet."

"I don't know what you're talking about." Now J.R. was the one who was irritated. "Violet's my best friend."

"Well, she's always with Ava these days, and I think she likes Matt Ghent."

"She does not!" J.R. protested. But she actually had no idea if Violet liked Matt. The thought had never occurred to her.

"Sorry," said Tommy. "I didn't mean to raise a sore subject. My mom told me that these things happen, and it doesn't mean you're not friends anymore."

J.R. didn't feel like taking advice from Tommy, never mind his mom. The bathrooms by the tennis courts where she usually changed were now in sight, and Miranda waved as she headed inside. Miranda's parents had organized a pizza dinner to celebrate the end of the season after their game on Sunday, and J.R. was looking forward to it. "I don't want to be late for practice," J.R. said, starting to jog toward the squat little building even though she knew Tommy was heading to the same place. When she got to the women's room door, she looked back. Tommy was dragging one foot through a pile of snow that was left beneath a lamppost. He was still eating his chips.

J.R. thought about her conversation with Tommy all through practice and the whole way home. He made it sound so easy to talk to his cousin. She wanted to talk to Violet, but questions were still swirling around in her head. As she passed by June's, she saw Alex and Maria with their heads bent together, looking at something on the counter with a customer beside them. J.R. couldn't tell who it was, but the woman looked a lot like Ms. Kline. Not wanting to get caught spying, J.R. took one more glance without success and kept walking. When she got to the apartment, she didn't bother changing out of her soccer clothes before she got out her journal and scribbled down some questions.

~ What's so great about Ava?
- Is Ava maybe not as bad as I think?
- Ava seems to like Curtis.
• At least he's kind of funny.

~ Does Violet really like Matt?
- How could she? He never talks.
~ Do Ava, Aria, and Adelaide think I'm not cool enough?
- I think I know the answer to that one....
- Or maybe Aria thinks I'm okay—poutine assignment was fun.
• Was she serious about French camp?
~ What about Violet? What does she think?

J.R. doodled a frowning face. Then she tried writing out some things she could actually ask Violet if she got up the nerve. Only one question came to mind:

Are we still best friends?

Chapter 24

"MY FEET ARE FREEZING!" VIOLET pulled off her socks and threw them next to her boots by the Fernandos' front door.

"It's forty-five degrees out. How cold can they be?"

"Cold enough that the only thing that will warm them up is a cup of hot chocolate!"

The girls giggled and headed to Violet's kitchen, where she filled the kettle with water and turned on the stove before taking two packets of hot chocolate mix out of the cupboard. Violet's mom was a huge fan of ice-skating and Christmas. Every year, she took the girls to the rink at Rockefeller Center on the Saturday of Thanksgiving weekend, and they had just arrived back home. Unlike the year before, when they had sleepovers constantly, this was the first time J.R. had even been to Violet's house since the start of sixth grade.

"So I found out something bad," J.R. said after they settled into Violet's room with their drinks. She hadn't meant to talk about Alex's dilemma, but in the comfort of Violet's room, it started to slip out.

Violet put her mug on the floor and lay down on her back. She planted her feet, knees in the air, on a white fake-fur rug that she had added to her room. "Uh-oh," Violet said. "What is it?"

"June's is closing. Someone bought the building and doesn't want the space to be a store anymore."

"That's terrible. When?"

"In March." *Or maybe not,* J.R. thought to herself, if she could find the right magazine to fix things. Despite Alex's warning, she definitely hadn't given up on the idea of helping him with a story.

"That's so unfair! We have to do something," Violet said. "June's is an institution. I mean, how many times did we go there when we were little? Every Saturday for how long? Plus, there are all those people they teach to read, and all the neighbors who go to buy books. Maybe we could start a petition. I bet every kid at Nic has been there, even Curtis." Violet laughed at her own joke. Curtis definitely didn't do a lot of voluntary reading. "Or what about writing to the *East Side Press*?"

That was a great idea! Violet had written similar letters with Nic's Endangered Species Club. J.R. did worry that Alex was quiet, and a letter could be loud. She wondered if he would like it. But after lots of people wrote to the neighborhood news site the year before, the city had agreed not to build on top of a nearby park, so letters could also be effective. And since it was impossible to say when Ms. Kline would put out a magazine cover that J.R. could use to rewrite June's fate, they could certainly try something else in the meantime. "Let's do it," she said. "Can we use your computer?"

Violet disappeared momentarily to retrieve her laptop. Then she plopped herself back on the rug with her back against the bed and motioned for J.R. to join her. They stared at the blank screen. "We need to sound serious," Violet said, "to make them take us seriously."

J.R. agreed, although she wondered if a letter that obviously came from two kids might actually be more persuasive. After all, everyone worried that young people never read books, so it could be extra powerful to prove them wrong. Preferring to keep up momentum, she deferred to Violet.

"Dear Ms. Lane," Violet typed into the body of an email. It was easy to remember the name of the *ESP* editor since it was truly Lois Lane, just like Superman's journalist girlfriend.

> It has come to our attention that a neighborhood institution is being shuttered: June's Bookstore, a mainstay of the Upper East Side for almost 25 years.

"Is that too dramatic?"

"I think it's good," J.R. said encouragingly. "Keep going."

> This would be a terrible, terrible loss for the community. For generations, children have learned to

love books at June's, and many adults have depended
on their literacy program as well.

June's is like Central Park, the Met, or Bart's Bagels.

J.R. laughed. Bart's always had a line out the door but
was hardly equivalent to the first two landmarks on the list;
nor, of course, was June's. "I think that's going a little too
far. What about, 'It's a place that has made so many people
happy, inspired readers and writers, and brought our community together.'"

"Love that!" Violet said. She read out loud as she continued typing.

Alex Richardson has created a place we all treasure.

We need to save June's Books. Please publish this
reader letter in solidarity with June's. We hope the
predatory landlord behind this will see what a loss this
would be for our community.

Violet typed their names at the bottom. "I really love it,"
she said. "Nice being writing partners with you."

"Nice being writing partners with you, too." They should
probably hit send on the email to Lois Lane, but it felt like the
right time to open up, and J.R. didn't want to lose her nerve.
She knew that Violet was good at keeping secrets, and J.R.

was sick of hiding hers entirely. "So," she said, "I've kind of been having a really unusual fall."

"What do you mean?"

Just then, Violet's phone rang. She retrieved it from her desk and climbed onto her bed. Then she listened, and occasionally she laughed.

J.R. didn't want to eavesdrop, but it was hard not to in such a small space. To occupy herself, she looked more closely around Violet's room. The rug wasn't the only new item. Violet had replaced her rainbow-and-cloud-covered comforter with a gray-and-white blanket, and she had hung a full-length mirror behind her door. Although she used to have a poster of a girl playing a cello above her desk, now there was a bulletin board with some photos of Violet and a bunch of girls wearing their green-and-white Wachusett uniforms. J.R. thought about the purple pony-covered quilt she had had since first grade. Maybe she would ask for a new one for Christmas, now that she didn't need to save her requests for a phone. When she couldn't pretend not to pay attention anymore, J.R. looked back at Violet and saw that her friend was blushing.

"Really?" Violet asked into the phone. "You think?" There were a few more giggles. "J.R.'s here so I have to go, but that's pretty cool. I guess I'll see you there!"

Violet hung up but didn't make a move to get off her bed. J.R. sat back down on the floor and asked, "What's up?"

"Curtis asked Ava to go to a Knicks game in a few weeks. She thinks that Matt is going to ask me to go, too. Isn't that cool? A double date, although Curtis's dad will be there to supervise. Apparently, he won the tickets in some kind of raffle. That's so lucky, right?"

J.R. had never heard of anyone from their class going on a date before. She wasn't surprised that Ava would be the first girl to get asked—or do the asking—but Violet never talked about boys in a dating kind of way. Plus, what would Violet and Matt talk about? He didn't seem to say much.

"So you're going to go?"

"Of course I'm going!" Violet exclaimed. "I mean, if he asks me." The previously put-away iPhone was now tucked right next to Violet's leg.

"You think your mom will let you?"

"My mom will totally let me." J.R. made a mental note to add first dates to the list of things that Violet's parents were more relaxed about than her own. "Have you heard about the dance?" Violet asked. Every year, the Nic Parents' Association hosted a sixth-grade dance right before winter break, but that was all J.R. knew. "Ava's mom is in charge of planning the whole thing."

"Do you think you'll go with Matt?"

"Not sure," Violet said. "I mean, it's not like you need a date to go, but it's probably fun to have one." *Great*, thought J.R., since she definitely wouldn't. "What were you saying about your unusual fall?" Violet tucked her hair behind her ear and smiled conspiratorially. "Is there something you haven't told me about you and Tommy?"

"What?" J.R. knitted her eyebrows into a "What's wrong with you?" face.

"You're always talking to him, and he got kind of cute over the summer, even with the braces. Then he showed up to Curtis's in that mobster costume after he knew you were going as a flapper. I mean, he definitely did that on purpose!"

The costume symmetry hadn't occurred to J.R., who wanted to move the conversation along. "I'm always talking to him because we sit next to each other."

"Whatever," said Violet, clearly not convinced. "So if it's not Tommy, what was so interesting about your fall?"

J.R. looked at her friend the way Ms. Kline often looked at J.R., like she was assessing the situation. Reassessing, really. Clearly J.R. had been wrong to almost-share her secret. "Nothing," she said instead. "Let's send that email."

Violet had picked up her phone, checking for a text from Matt already. "Let me read it one more time," she said. "I don't want there to be any typos. Plus, my dad says it's rude to send work emails on the weekend, so it's probably better if I send it Monday morning before school."

J.R. wasn't worried about it being rude to send the email, and she hadn't seen any typos as they composed the message. But she had clearly lost Violet's attention. Rather than argue, she let it go. There was probably no difference between Saturday and Monday, anyway. "Want to watch a movie?" she proposed.

"Sure," said Violet. "Ava told me about some really funny romantic comedies on Netflix," she continued. "Let's take a look."

Chapter 25

J.R. WALKED INTO SCHOOL ON Monday morning at the same time as Violet. "Did you send it?" she asked. Violet held the door to the stairs but didn't answer. When a group of seventh graders pushed by, she fell behind without a fight. Two flights up, J.R. stopped on the landing to wait. "The *East Side Press* publishes their letters to the editor on Fridays. Alex will be so surprised—hopefully his landlord reads it, too." J.R. realized that Violet wasn't reacting with even a fraction of the enthusiasm she had shown on Saturday night. In fact, she wasn't reacting at all. "You sent our email, right?"

"Not exactly." Violet looked straight down at the floor.

"Why not?"

"I thought about it—" Violet stammered. J.R. saw a hint of water pooling in Violet's eyes. "I thought about it, and maybe it isn't something we should get involved in."

"What do you mean not something we should get involved in? We're talking about June's! A neighborhood landmark, remember?" Kids streaming by barely noticed J.R.'s escalating volume.

"I know I said that stuff. But if someone bought the building, and they want to do something else with it, maybe we're out of our depths." Violet looked so distraught that J.R. started to feel bad for her despite her betrayal. "Besides, I'm sure Alex can find another spot. My mom's always saying how sad it is that there are so many empty storefronts in the neighborhood." The hopeful look on Violet's face didn't convince J.R. that another location was a viable solution, and Violet didn't look convinced, either.

"That is absolutely not the point and you know it," J.R. said. "June's isn't any old store in any old space. It's the wooden bookcases, and the ladder, and George sunning himself in the window."

"I know," Violet confessed. She took the back of her right hand and pressed it to the corner of her eye. "But I'm just not sure if we should be the ones leading the charge. Or at least I shouldn't. It could be better coming from you now that you're such good friends with Alex. I have to return a book," she said, grasping for an excuse to veer off toward the library. "I'll see you upstairs."

J.R.'s stomach formed a knot. She couldn't understand why Violet had changed her mind. Not only had they just unraveled all the progress the two of them had made, but her plan to help Alex was dissolving before it even began. Did Violet have a point that it wasn't their business? J.R. couldn't think clearly in the stairwell with all the kids pushing by. Instead, she headed to class, grateful for once that her desk wasn't next to Violet's. When she got to the room, a substitute teacher was there. Ms. Kline was out sick.

"Can anyone help me with this?" The sub struggled with Ms. Kline's cabinet while trying to read a piece of paper.

"The secret files!" Curtis came to the teacher's aid and yanked open the drawer with more force than was necessary.

"I think I've got it now," she scolded. "Ms. Kline asked me to give you this assignment. I'm going to put out these magazine covers," she said as she skimmed the sheet, which looked like a printout of her email, "and you are each going to pick one and write whatever comes to mind. Fast. The instructions say I should make clear that what you write doesn't have to be perfect. Your teacher wants you to speed-write, stream-of-consciousness style." Violet finally got to the room as the sub finished displaying the cover options. She looked a little puzzled by Ms. Kline's absence. "Okay, everyone," the sub said. "Go!"

Like the running of the bulls in Pamplona, the students raced from their desks. Something about being told to write fast made even the least inclined get excited. J.R. tripped and fell in the shuffle, slamming her palms into the linoleum floor so hard she wanted to cry. It wasn't just the pain, but the combination of her stinging hands, her frustration with Violet, and her worry about June's converging all at once. While she was still on the ground, Curtis tripped over her. Rather than apologizing, he looked back and glared. Out of nowhere, Tommy appeared to help her up and ask if she was okay. J.R. blinked her eyes twice to stop the tears before saying she was fine.

Tommy waited for J.R. to collect herself, which was all the time it took for the class to decimate the sub's selection. When they got to the far window, there were only two covers left. One was a picture of a quarterback calling out a play to his huddled teammates. It was drawn from below, looking up at a ring of broad shoulders and helmet-covered faces. The other showed an unmanned newsstand on a rainy New York street. The artist had muted the normal colors of the magazines and candy bars so that they were almost as drab as the cloudy sky and puddle-covered street. Neither drawing appealed to J.R., but the newsstand was downright depressing. How much more could she take?

"You first," J.R. said, knowing Tommy would choose the football picture. He was even wearing a blue Jason Storrs Giants jersey. Storrs was hardly a star—in fact, he'd barely played after dropping two key passes at the very beginning of the season—but Tommy liked the Giants' unsung rookie. For the last three weeks, he hadn't stopped talking about how his grandfather was taking him to the Giants-Jets game that coming weekend. The Jets were having a much better season, but Tommy insisted his team would win, and J.R. admired his spirit. It was good to have faith in the underdog, and of course a Giants victory would be good for her dad, too.

To J.R.'s surprise, Tommy swallowed visibly, then picked up the newsstand picture. "Not sure why," he said, "but I'm feeling up for a challenge."

"That's really taking one for the team, pun intended." The joke lifted J.R.'s spirits.

"You mean punt intended?" Tommy looked pretty satisfied with his own quip.

Back at her desk, J.R. wondered if she should have insisted on giving Tommy the football cover, especially since he was staring dejectedly at his page rather than writing. She started to propose a switch when the sub announced that they had five minutes left. She drew a deep breath and began to scribble. Time to go for it.

> "Run!" I screamed. "You've got this!"
> My grandfather was also screaming, but he wasn't as polite.

J.R. went through naming options in her head before making a decision to keep things simple. Jason Storrs became a fictional James, and the Giants' quarterback became Leo.

> James was all alone. I seriously have no idea how he broke away like that, but he did. It was an unbelievable move for anyone, especially a rookie.
> Unfortunately, now he was about to make an actual rookie mistake. He had gotten so far so

fast, and now it practically looked like he was
running for the end zone—without the ball.

If James just turned around, he would see
Leo watching him, seeing the opening, bringing
his arm back to throw.

But if he kept going, he'd just be on the
fastest, longest, most useless breakaway in history.

J.R. chuckled. She'd give Tommy the result he wanted, but
not without a little messiness first.

"Turn around!" I shouted. And let me tell
you, I wasn't the only one shouting. "You gotta
turn around! That ball is yours! It's your
moment, James!"

And then he heard me! I swear he heard
me—specifically, me—telling him to turn. I
mean, he was directly in front of me even if
our seats weren't exactly close to the field. But
we made eye contact. I know it. I could see the
whites of his eyes through his helmet, even. And
then he turned his torso and launched himself
into the air. Arms up, hands ready, ball heading
straight towa—

"Done!" the sub announced cheerily. "Everyone put your
pencils down."

J.R. added "rd him." to complete the sentence. She tried to keep writing but got called out. "That includes you." The teacher started to collect the papers, taking J.R.'s first. In her rush to get started, J.R. hadn't included a title, but now the perfect one came to mind: "Mind Meld of Unsung Champions."

"Do you feel your creative juices flowing?" the sub asked.

"I do!" Ava answered without raising her hand. J.R. wondered what Ava had been writing about with such enthusiasm. "Do we get to finish these tonight?"

"No, that's it for this assignment. Ms. Kline wanted everyone to put pens to paper and spit something out. Sometimes it's interesting to see what happens when you don't have time to worry about getting things just right."

Maybe, J.R. thought, but she wasn't so sure. This time, she knew exactly the ending she had in mind: She wanted James to catch the ball and get to the end zone. That would make Tommy very, very happy.

Chapter 26

"IT WAS LIKE HE HEARD me yelling in the crowd!" Tommy called to Curtis across the classroom while they unpacked their bags one week later. "I was shouting, 'Turn around! Turn around!' 'cause I could see the whole play unfolding right in front of me. And then he did! Jason turned around, and he saw the ball flying at him. It was a perfect spiral and then poof!" Tommy signaled an explosion with his hands. "The thing just dropped like a brick. The ball defied the laws of physics."

J.R. wasn't totally sure what the laws of physics were and doubted Tommy knew, either, but she understood exactly what he was talking about. The mysteriously falling ball was all over the news the night before. J.R. had watched the play over and over again online, chuckling as the announcers struggled to understand the incomplete pass that fell from the sky.

"Incomplete" was definitely a fitting description, J.R. thought, just like her story.

Despite the missed catch—or short pass, depending on your perspective—Jason Storrs had ended the game a hero. With three seconds left, a Hail Mary pass floated into his outstretched hands, and he ran the ball into the end zone to score the winning touchdown. Tommy was ecstatic. He vowed to wear his Storrs jersey every day until the Super Bowl. J.R. worried he would actually do it.

The sad part was that the player Jason outran was in his thirteenth year in the league and, after the game, announced he would retire. His bad back was acting up, and it simply wasn't worth it. He hated leaving on a loss, he said, but he had to do it. J.R. wished there was some way she could make amends. It was awesome to see Tommy so happy, but she really didn't like the losses that weighed against the wins.

In contrast to Tommy's elation, Violet looked extremely unhappy as they headed to music.

"Still nothing?" Ava whispered while she held the classroom door. Violet shook her head.

"That stinks." Adelaide's comment sounded more provocative than sympathetic, and Ava cut her off with a look.

J.R. kind of wondered what they were talking about and kind of didn't care. She was still so unhappy with Violet for abandoning their plan that it was hard to muster too much sympathy. If her friend wouldn't help, J.R. did need to act on her own to help June's, but she was having trouble coming up with a plan. Sending the *East Side Press* an email alone wasn't appealing. She had promised Alex she wouldn't use a magazine to try to fix his problems, so that was out even though it was so tempting. Ms. Kline hadn't given any new *Gothamite* assignments since she got back from being sick anyway, so it wasn't really an option. It almost felt like she was holding out on purpose. In the meantime, J.R. worried about Alex. Whenever she stopped by the store, which she did more often knowing that her days there might now be limited, he seemed distracted and something about the place felt off. Even George was acting funny. He hadn't swatted at J.R. in weeks.

"Can't you reason with them?" she asked when she visited June's after school and raised the subject of the lease.

"Those lawyers are tough, and the landlord's a new guy who bought the building a couple of years back," Alex said. "I've never even met him. I hope we'll find a solution, but we'll just have to see. Either way, I think it's probably time for some changes."

"I still don't understand," J.R. said, "why you can't solve this with a magazine, or why you won't let me try. What's so special about grown-up problems that a *Gothamite* story can't fix?"

"Ah," Alex said, taking in J.R.'s confusion. He pulled out two stools tucked behind the counter so both of them could sit. "For one thing, it's not my turn with the magazines anymore. Those are for kids like you and your own challenges, and for Kate to work with."

"Then I'll ask her to help! Or I'll do it myself if you'll let me. I just need Ms. Kline to give out another assignment." For as much as J.R. wanted to help Alex, her pleas were slightly selfish, too. If Alex gave up, if he simply closed the store, she would miss their time together enormously, she realized.

"Leave it alone, J.R." Alex said it nicely, not like a scolding, but there was no doubt he was serious. "You've got your own work to do. I want you to stay focused."

"Focused on what?"

"Focused on what Kate's trying to teach you. That's important. Maria?" Alex called out and cut off the conversation. Maria emerged from the office. "I need to get a little air. Do you mind watching the front for a minute?"

"Not at all. You want to help me clean up the picture books?" Maria asked.

J.R. didn't really want to, but she couldn't say no. Alex usually kept the place pristine. It was surprising that he hadn't noticed some kid had emptied two shelves of books onto the floor. Somehow, J.R. needed to make things right.

J.R. helped Maria as quickly as she could. If she hurried, Ms. Kline might still be at Nic, since teachers often stayed late to finish their work. When the last book was back on the shelves, J.R. ran all the way back to school and up the stairs to the sixth floor, where she was relieved to find her teacher.

"J.R.?" Ms. Kline looked up from the papers she was grading as her student flew through the door.

J.R. didn't even try to be subtle about catching her breath. She took two big gulps of air before launching in. "I need your help. And Alex does, too."

Ms. Kline raised her eyebrows.

"May I sit down?" J.R. asked. Without waiting for an answer, she plopped down opposite Ms. Kline. "I know you know Alex," she said. There was no reaction from her teacher. "You probably already knew that since you seem to know everything."

"Not everything," Ms. Kline interjected.

"But you know enough to help him. You have to. You have to save June's, or at least give me a *Gothamite* cover so I can do it."

"Hasn't Alex talked to you about this? He's quite good at explaining things, don't you think? I'd say he's got a knack for it."

"Yes, he told me he can't use the covers, but he also said he doesn't want my help!" Again Ms. Kline did not respond. "Fine," J.R. said. "Point taken. He doesn't want my help. But what about yours? Can't you do something for a fellow member of your alumni network?"

Ms. Kline cocked her head slightly. "That's a rather specific term."

J.R. realized she had messed up. She hoped her nosiness didn't derail her plea for help. "I peeked," she confessed. "Or I snooped, really, in your file cabinet. I found the letter from Eleanor Mendell." The pieces were coming together. "And I know you know Alex, and she was also his teacher, and now I'm guessing that somehow he sent you to me?" J.R. wasn't totally sure the last part was true, but it felt right.

"That's all correct. Alex called me this summer after a certain spilled-coffee incident? He thought that you needed some help, and I had an unexpected opening in my schedule so I was able to oblige."

Able to oblige was such a Ms. Kline thing to say. Not *so I came straight away* or *I was happy to do it*. "But if Alex won't let me do it, you need to help him!"

"That's not my job, or yours."

"But I want to!"

The corners of Ms. Kline's lips started to quiver, tempted to arch upward. "Please don't get between Alex and his concerns, J.R. He needs to make his own decisions. But there are other ways you can show your support, even if he does decide to close June's. Why don't you give that some thought, and I'll see you back in class tomorrow?" Ms. Kline tilted her head toward the door. J.R. had been dismissed.

Chapter 27

J.R. STILL COULDN'T GO HOME. She had too many thoughts swirling around and needed to clear her head. It was getting late, but there was something she wanted to see. She headed to Albertine.

Walking down Madison Avenue to 79th Street, J.R. looked at the stores with elaborate holiday window displays, then turned right toward Fifth Avenue and the Gilded Age mansion on the corner, with a facade covered in arched windows and stone columns. J.R. wondered why she had never noticed it before. Inside, she passed through security and walked toward the back, where a crowd was entering. J.R. was the only kid there and tried to blend in as she followed them upstairs, where Aria had said she'd find the ceiling mural. It was even more amazing than J.R. had expected.

While most of the visitors veered left toward a reading, J.R. sat down in one of the brown leather chairs surrounded by shelves of French books. She tipped her head up toward the ceiling, which was painted a deep blue and covered in gold stars. Each planet from the solar system was pictured in its place, and the artist had painted all the signs of the zodiac on top of a big black ring around the center. J.R. would always be loyal to June's, but this was probably the coolest bookstore she had ever seen. She sat for a while, stargazing in the middle of Manhattan, until she heard the audience clap. It reminded her that it was time to get home.

In the lobby, J.R. stopped for one more look around on her way out. A small marble statue stood on a pedestal in front of the door, a young archer flanked by turtles and missing his arms. He had curly hair and no clothes. The statue must have been very old.

"Do you know his story?" The woman who approached J.R. was about Ms. Kline's age and had a distinct French accent. J.R. couldn't see the name on her badge, but the ID pinned to her sweater suggested that she worked there. She probably wondered what J.R. was doing in the building on her own.

"No," J.R. said. "I've never been here before. I didn't even realize I could come in."

"We wish more people knew they could come in!" the woman said. "As for the statue, it's a replica of a work by Michelangelo. The original is on loan at the Metropolitan Museum."

"Really?" J.R. asked as she slid around to look at the boy head-on. The statue didn't look familiar, although the style was definitely one she had seen before. The Met was full of marble statues of people and angels, a lot of them as naked as this boy was.

"Yes, the original is called *Cupid*. It was brought to the United States at the beginning of the twentieth century, around the time this house was built. It was on display right here for many years without anyone knowing its provenance. Then a professor from New York University came by, and she realized what a treasure we had on our hands. Eventually, we loaned it to the museum."

The woman kept talking, but J.R. didn't hear the rest of what she said. She couldn't believe the first part—a marble statue by Michelangelo had been discovered in the building, hiding in plain sight just down the street from the Met. It was a real-life *Mixed-Up Files*, but instead of Angel, this Michelangelo was called *Cupid*.

"Excuse me," J.R. interrupted. "When did the professor discover the statue? Was it a long time ago?"

"Not too long. It was in the mid-1990s."

That was even more amazing. It meant that when E. L. Konigsburg came up with her story in the 1960s, she had no idea how almost-true it was. J.R. wasn't sure who to tell first. She could text Aria, since she never would have discovered the coincidence if Aria hadn't told her about Albertine. She could call Violet because the *Mixed-Up Files* was a book they both loved and shared. Or she could run home and tell Alex, who would appreciate every detail, too.

But then it dawned on her that she didn't want to tell anyone. She wanted to sit with her secret, at least for now. J.R. thanked the woman for letting her know about *Cupid* and walked back out onto Fifth Avenue. She paused several blocks north in front of the Met. All J.R. could think was that there were so many treasures inside, and so many more to discover.

Chapter 28

WHEN J.R. WALKED INTO THE Nic lobby on Wednesday morning, someone had hung a huge glitter-covered banner announcing that the sixth-grade dance would be on the last night of school before winter break. That was less than two weeks away. J.R. considered the poem in her backpack. Their latest assignment had been to write a haiku about a conversation between two people. Ms. Kline told them to make each word count, since a haiku had to include only and exactly seventeen syllables, with five on the first line, seven in the middle, and five again on the third. J.R., following Ms. Kline's and Alex's advice not to get involved with June's, had picked a *Gothamite* cover with two women sitting on a park bench and drafted a poem in which they decided to get their daughter a puppy. It was pretty clever, although J.R. was still wary of the damaging domino effect her stories could have. Her haiku went:

She convinced her wife
To get a dog for their girl
A cute one, of course

Looking at the banner, J.R. questioned her decision. Maybe she should have used the assignment differently. She ran through some possible opening lines in her head, counting out the required five syllables.

Dance with me, J.R.?

First dance, let's go, yay!

He asked, she smiled, yes!

"So, are you going?" Tommy asked, passing by on his way to the stairs.

"I don't know." J.R. blushed as if he had read her thoughts. She repeated Tommy's question in her head and counted his own coincidental five-syllable sentence. "I guess I'll think about it."

"I was wondering, um, I kind of wanted to ask—"

Before Tommy could finish wondering, Ava walked up. "Hey, guys," she said. "Like my sign? I helped my mom paint it, and the glitter made a huge mess! My mom said about a thousand times that it was more than she bargained for."

"Looks good," said Tommy. Spotting Curtis, he left the girls abruptly.

"What do you think?" Ava beckoned to Violet, who looked like she would have rather gone straight to the stairs.

"The banner looks really good. But I don't have a date, so I'm not sure I'll go." Violet didn't exactly turn her back on J.R., but she didn't completely include her, either. They still hadn't talked since their argument, and the longer their silence went on, the harder it got to break.

"Don't be silly," said Ava. "You don't need a date. It'll be cool no matter what."

Violet looked skeptical. J.R. stayed silent.

A few hours later, their class was in the library. Mr. Kasselbaum, the middle school librarian, spent the first half of the period discussing research techniques for their upcoming study of immigration, and then he sent them off to pick books. Normally, J.R. loved that type of assignment, but today she didn't feel like browsing. She had seen a book about the Triangle Shirtwaist Factory fire on display by the computers, and she checked it out without looking at any other options. Then she settled into a beanbag chair to read.

"Nice work, right?" J.R. heard Adelaide's voice from behind a nearby bookshelf.

"You have to be quiet," Aria responded at a more library-appropriate volume.

"All it took was a few comments about how she lugs around that cello for Matt to get it. Why are you looking at me like that?"

"I don't know," Aria whispered. "It just—" It was possible she swallowed, or at least J.R. imagined hearing a gulp. "It just seems mean, don't you think? And actually—"

"Come on," Adelaide chided. "I'm sick of Violet clinging to Ava."

J.R. didn't like the sound of this at all. There had to be a story she could write to confront the girls. A *Gothamite* cover came to mind, one that had a group of preschool-age kids sitting in a circle on a rug. The boys flung themselves in all directions. The girls, all dressed in blue shirts and red hair scarves, looked at one another with conviction and flexed their arms like Rosie the Riveter. If Ms. Kline put that one out again, J.R. could get pumped up.

"What are you guys talking about?" Ava's question brought J.R. back to the library.

"What do you mean?" Aria's voice shook slightly.

"She means, what were you guys talking about?" J.R. stood up and revealed herself. There was no debated decision, only a change of plans. She wasn't going to wait around for a magazine to help her say what she wanted to say. "Did you do something to mess up Violet's date with Matt?" In that moment, it didn't matter how frustrated she was with her friend for backing out of their plans, or for backing away, if J.R. were honest, from their friendship. J.R. wasn't going to let Adelaide hurt Violet without speaking up.

"I just told him she's a dork," Adelaide sneered. "Kind of like you."

"That's the worst you can do?" When J.R. challenged Adelaide's unimaginative barb, Aria took a step back. "Why would you go out of your way to be mean to someone?"

The question caught Adelaide off guard. Instead of answering, she turned to Ava. "You didn't listen when we told you that Violet's dull, but Matt wasn't hard to convince." J.R. could believe that. Matt didn't show any sign of having a personality.

"Then he's as bad as you are," Ava shot back.

"You know why Violet won't help you save that bookstore, right?" Adelaide turned squarely toward J.R., who definitely did not know the answer. "She came over to Ava's the day after you two wrote your email. She told us all about how terrible it was that some landlord was making the place close, and how you were going to save the day." Adelaide stopped, making J.R. wait for the big, terrible reveal. "Until she found out that Ava's dad is the one kicking them out."

J.R. hated the look of satisfaction on Adelaide's face. "Is that true?"

"Yeah," Ava answered very, very softly. "My dad bought the building, and he wants to put a restaurant in. He says he can charge a lot more rent."

"And you told Violet?"

"Uh-huh. I'm really sorry. I feel really ba—"

"And," J.R. interrupted, then couldn't finish the rest. *And she sided with you.* Rather than continue, J.R. simply walked away. She found a spot in the window and sat by herself for the rest of the period. There was no one at all she wanted to talk to. There was nothing else to say.

The school day couldn't end quickly enough. J.R. avoided Violet all afternoon and walked home as fast as she could. She tried to do her homework, but solving math problems was the last thing she'd be able to focus on. She really didn't care whether Jacob, who started sixth grade at exactly 5 feet 2 inches tall on September 1 and grew 0.3 inches per month, was taller on March 1 than Michael, who started sixth grade at 5 feet 1 inch tall and grew 0.45 inches per month. J.R. was mad, and she wanted to confront Violet. Sort of.

She picked up her phone and typed a stream-of-consciousness message.

> I don't get it, Violet. I thought you loved June's and we had a plan. And now you just gave up because Ava's dad owns the building (yeah, Adelaide told me)? That hurts. I thought we were friends, but I guess Ava, and even her father, come first.

J.R. debated whether to add something about Adelaide and Matt. She wanted to, but it would just be out of spite. She decided to end there and hit send.

Three flashing dots appeared as Violet typed a response.

But when the message came through it wasn't from Violet. It was Curtis.

> I didn't know Violet loved June's (what's June?). I thought she loved Matt. Too bad he likes Adelaide more.

J.R. had accidentally written to the group chat. A cold wave ran through her whole body. She waited a second and created a new message. J.R. double-checked that it really was going to just Violet. "I'm sorry," it said, but no one wrote back.

Chapter 29

As soon as she woke up, J.R. told her mom she didn't feel well and needed to stay home. Without a fever, her plea completely failed. As J.R. dragged herself into school, she was still debating whether to find Violet and apologize, find Violet and yell at her, or just leave Violet alone.

"What happened?" Tommy asked when they got to their desks.

"I don't want to talk about it." J.R. snuck a look at Violet, who was writing in her planner even though Ms. Kline hadn't even started class, never mind given out any new assignments. Then J.R. looked toward Adelaide, who was smiling. "I really, really don't."

"Okay," Tommy said. "I get it."

But he didn't get it, of course. No one did. J.R. felt humiliated. And even though she was mad at Violet, she definitely hadn't meant for her friend to find out about Matt and Adelaide that way. Everything was terrible.

J.R. busied herself with unpacking. When she handed in her math homework, her teacher lowered her voice and tried to console her. "It's all right, J.R. Remember what I told you. The stories aren't miracle solutions—you can't just make good things happen, like getting a phone, without something bad happening, too." She gave J.R. a pointed look that was also sympathetic. "But you can fix this," she said. "You don't need magic to do it. Look inside yourself. That's what the magazines are for. They're about what you want to make happen, not what's happening to you."

Ms. Kline's words stuck with J.R. for the rest of the day. She tried looking inside herself, but was anything useful in there? During lunch, she skipped the cafeteria and went straight to the library, wanting to be alone and also unable to imagine sitting in the same room as everyone else when she couldn't hide behind the structure of her teachers' lessons. But when she got there, all she could think about was how strongly she had felt her convictions when standing up to Adelaide, and how much it hurt when she found out that Violet hadn't had her back in remotely the same way.

When school ended, J.R. headed home but didn't hurry. Maria was in June's window putting up garlands and placing a menorah on one of the shelves that normally held a book. Alex had finally hung a sign on the door announcing their holiday party, the weekend after next, which was doubling as June's twenty-fifth-birthday celebration. There was no mention of it likely being the last. Alex had taken so long to post the date that J.R. worried he didn't have the heart to host this year at all, so it was a relief to see he was up for some festivities. From inside the window, Maria waved as George charged his head into her leg. She bent down to scratch behind his ears and motioned for J.R. to come in. Still not ready for company, J.R. mouthed, "Next time," and turned back, away from home. Even though her apartment normally felt like a good place to retreat, she needed some time to think, and she knew where she wanted to do it. J.R. turned toward the Met.

There was a short line at security before J.R. could check her backpack. Then she asked for an admission sticker from the members' desk. The woman at the counter asked if she needed a map, but J.R. already had her destination in mind. She knew how to get to Bubbles's Bedroom, where she was guaranteed some peace and quiet. As she started to go, she realized she did have one question.

"Do you know where I can find Michelangelo's statue called *Cupid*?"

"Hmm," the woman said. "I don't but I'll look." Seeing the statue would be so redeeming, J.R. was sure. She wished she had kept her phone so she could take a photo, but it was checked with her bag. "Unfortunately, it doesn't look like *Cupid* is on display at the moment. If you would like, I can print you out a page about the work."

The disappointing news brought her emotions up from right below the surface, where they had been swimming. Wiping away a tear while trying to be subtle, she thanked the woman for the offer but declined. J.R. set out for Bubbles's Bedroom, trying to get to the serene and familiar space as fast as she could.

When she got there, J.R. drew a sharp breath as she realized that her bad luck would continue. There was never anyone in the gallery, but today of all days, someone was already sitting by the window. When that someone turned around, J.R. saw it was Violet.

"Hi." Her friend sounded tired but not surprised by the coincidence.

"What are you doing here?" J.R. asked.

"I needed to think." J.R. suppressed a smile. It was comforting to know they'd had the same instinct. "I figured this was the best place I could go to be by myself."

J.R. wasn't sure what to make of the second part of Violet's answer, which undid the comfort. "Should I go?" she asked. She definitely wasn't there to antagonize her friend.

"No, don't," Violet said. "I meant that I expected to be by myself when I came here, but I'm glad I'm not." She scooted over to make room.

"I'm really sorry," J.R. said after neither girl spoke for a while. "I shouldn't have texted all that stuff. I didn't mean it. I mean, I did mean the part about why I was upset, but I wasn't trying to tell everyone."

"It's fine." Violet shrugged. "And I'm sorry about June's. Ava called when she saw Curtis's message and told me everything. I heard you really stood up for me with Adelaide."

Violet paused. "I was at Ava's house, and I told her and Adelaide that June's lost its lease and about the email we wrote. But then Ava explained how her dad had bought the building. I started to feel like maybe it wasn't our place to get involved."

J.R. looked at Violet. "That's all?"

"No," Violet admitted. She took a few seconds to finish. "And I didn't want to make Ava upset."

"But you didn't mind upsetting me," J.R. whispered.

Violet stared at her lap. Then she raised her head and her voice. "I'm sorry," she said. "I'm really, really sorry. I should probably go home."

"Wait," J.R. said quickly. She thought about how Tommy had been brave enough to talk to his cousin, and about how Alex told her to fight for her friend. She thought about Ms. Kline, who was trying to help her even if J.R. wasn't exactly sure how. She thought about sitting there with Violet, who had just apologized, and about how she wanted their friendship to stay the same, but how it was okay if it changed, too. She realized how much she would regret it if she let Violet leave without saying more.

"I know we haven't had the best fall—as friends, I mean."

Violet glanced toward the glass deer before saying, "Maybe." J.R. knew that "maybe," in this instance, was a concession.

"When you came back from camp, I was jealous." J.R. swallowed as she forced out the word. She was trying to be honest, so she needed to say it. "You were so excited to hang out with Ava, and with Aria and Adelaide."

"Ava's a really good friend," said Violet. "She's funny, and she likes to do lots of different stuff that I think you would like, too, if you gave it a try. She and her brother found this waterfall near the top of Central Park that I've never seen before, and she makes these hilarious TikTok videos that are so over the top. You'd love them."

J.R. nodded to show that she was at least open to the idea of appreciating Ava's talents, which had the benefit of being true. That wasn't something she could have said just a few months ago. Still, she hadn't meant to turn the conversation to anyone else. She needed to talk about how she felt. "I guess my feelings got hurt," she admitted. "I wasn't sure if you still wanted to be friends, and I wished things could be like they used to be." Before she could stop herself, J.R. added, "We're still friends, right?"

"Of course!" said Violet. "I've just liked doing new stuff, and I could tell you didn't want to give Ava a chance." J.R. started to protest, but Violet gave her a "let's be serious" look. "Like I said, I knew you didn't want to give her a chance but she's nice, I promise."

It was so tempting to agree and move on, but J.R. hadn't come this far not to follow through. She made herself keep going. "I believe you," she said. "I like Ava more than I thought I would. But I wasn't really talking about Ava. I mean, the problem wasn't really that you were hanging out with her; it was that you weren't hanging out with me."

J.R. followed Violet's gaze out the window and down toward the Temple of Dendur. Light coming through the wall of rectangular glass panes cast shadows on the pool of water at the end of the room, reminding J.R. of shimmering graph paper. "I guess sometimes I just wanted to do different things from what we were always doing together, and"—Violet hesitated—"sometimes I still might want to do separate stuff."

J.R. took a little breath. She did it quietly enough that Violet wouldn't hear, but it bought her a second to think. "I know," she said. "I've thought a lot about it, and now I see that being friends doesn't mean we have to be each other's *only* friend, or do everything together, or like all the same things—I guess." Both girls laughed sheepishly. "I've been thinking about camp next summer, too. I was really set on going to Wachusett, but Aria told me about this French writing camp here in New York and asked me to go with her. Then maybe I'll find something else to do after that. A sleepaway camp if my parents will let me."

Violet would never say so directly, but J.R. was sure that Violet was glad to have her space for the summer, even if she was willing to share it with Ava. "I'm glad you found me here," Violet said. "And I'm glad you said all that."

"I'm glad I did, too." Violet gave J.R. a hug. "I saw a painting that I think you'll like in the European galleries. Alex showed it to me, actually. Want to see?"

"Sure!" Violet answered with her old enthusiasm. "What is it?" J.R. explained about Sibylle and the X-ray. Violet was, indeed, impressed. "Very cool," she said as she studied the painting a few minutes later. "Very, very cool."

Chapter 30

WHEN J.R. GOT HOME, SHE felt better than she had in a long time. She was literally whistling as she let herself into the apartment. But when she dropped her bag in her room, there was something she didn't hear, the sound of Alex's fountain. Peeking out her window, she saw him, home early from June's, kneeling by the frog and shutting it down for the winter.

J.R. knew her day wasn't done. There still had to be a way to support her neighbor—Ms. Kline had made clear, to the extent she could even be clear, that the magazines weren't the only way. J.R. had an idea, although it would require reaching out to people in a way J.R. definitely wasn't used to. Hopefully, she could follow through. She told herself she didn't have a choice.

Picking up her phone, J.R. called Violet and was relieved when her friend answered right away. She explained her plan, and Violet agreed to help on one condition: J.R. had to tell

Ava first. That didn't sound fun, but it did sound fair. Violet thought she could do it by text, which seemed easier for J.R. and Ava both, so she got started.

JRS: YT?

AA: Yep.

JRS: I want to do something nice for Alex, June's owner. I don't think your dad will be mad but I wanted to tell you first.

AA: OK...What?

JRS: I'm going to make him a book, with Violet, with notes from people who like the store. Kids from our class, and people like that, to celebrate June's 25th birthday. Maybe it will inspire him to at least talk to your dad about some kind of arrangement. Or maybe it'll at least make him happy.

It took forever for Ava to respond. J.R.'s stomach clenched into a knot while she waited. Even though the notes were meant to be celebratory, not "Please help save June's," the whole project would probably still be a little awkward for Ava. Finally, the next message came through.

AA: Sorry, my mom was calling. But guess what! My dad renewed the lease. He got home early and just told me. Asked me if I ever shopped there, and I said honestly, no, but I know some kids who do. 😊

JRS: REALLY??

AA: Really.

This, J.R. thought, must be what it meant to experience a wave of relief. She typed the words "thank you" about a million times, until Ava reminded her that there was nothing to thank her for. Alex had somehow convinced her dad. J.R. wished she knew what he said, and what inspired him to do it, but the important thing was that it had all worked out. She called Violet to report the breaking news.

"Awesome!" Violet said after J.R. brought her up to speed. "The only thing is that I was kind of looking forward to our letter-writing campaign."

That's when J.R. realized that she was, too.

So the girls made a plan. It would still be nice to give Alex lots of notes to celebrate June's anniversary, probably even more so now that the store's future was secure. Right then on the phone, they worked out a list of people to ask: kids from their class; Ms. Kline; Mr. Kasselbaum, the librarian; and Maria, of course, who could probably help contact people from the adult literacy class, too. Violet lived in a big apartment building where she could put up a sign to solicit letters, and they were sure their parents would contribute, too. They didn't have much time if they wanted to get the present to Alex before the party.

"Want me to take care of the school part?" Violet asked, knowing that J.R. wasn't a big fan of asking her classmates for favors.

J.R. thought for a second. "That's all right," she said. "I'll do it."

J.R. found she didn't even mind asking her classmates to write to Alex. It was actually kind of fun. She didn't approach them all, of course, just the ones she thought might be interested. But even Margaret had something nice to say about how Alex had recommended a really good book about a women's baseball league, and Tommy wrote all about how Alex had helped him find the perfect history of the Miracle on Ice for his cousin.

J.R. didn't stop there. With Ms. Kline's help, she tracked down Harry Collins, who had drawn the *Gothamite* wedding picture, and Maria reached out to the Sunday morning reading group as well as George's vet, who was a fan of June's gardening section. Violet managed to get five letters from her neighbors and a couple of drawings from kids who came to the Saturday story hour. When they were done, Ms. Kline helped them assemble the letters into a nice book.

After about a week, the collection was ready. J.R. was, too. On Saturday morning, she brought the book to June's.

Hopefully, Alex would be there. She had stopped by a few times to tell him about her talk with Violet and let him tell her the news about the lease, but each time Maria said he was out. It almost felt like he was avoiding her. When she got there with the wrapped present in hand, Maria was on her way to pick up some final decorations for the party. Alex was alone by the cash register.

"Happy almost-twenty-fifth birthday!" J.R. said after the bells over the door finished jangling.

"Why, thank you." Alex glanced up from whatever he had been writing.

"Violet and I made you a present." J.R. walked to the back and handed Alex the box.

"Violet, eh?"

"Yep, we talked." J.R. filled Alex in on their reconciliation at the Met and how much better she felt. She even told him how close she'd come to not telling Violet how she really felt, but how she had made herself do it, and how that might have been the best part of all.

"I'm proud of you," Alex said. "It takes a lot to be honest about your feelings like that."

For once, J.R. knew exactly what he meant. She accepted the compliment gladly.

"Shall I open this?" Alex asked, motioning to the gift that J.R. had placed temptingly on the counter. He carefully tore off the wrapping paper, took out the book, and began to flip through it.

"This," he said, "is the best birthday present June's has ever gotten."

"Probably the only one," she countered.

"Don't diminish your efforts." Alex continued to look through the letters. He smiled when he got to a drawing of a jack-o'-lantern that one of the little kids had done. There was no person, and no book, anywhere in the picture, just a big scribbled pumpkin that must have really made an impression. "You arranged all this?"

"Yep." J.R. could hear the pride in her voice.

"What a note to end on," Alex whispered to himself, but not quietly enough for J.R. to miss it.

"End on? But I know!" This was getting ridiculous, J.R. thought. It was time to celebrate the news. "I heard from Ava that her dad renewed the lease!"

"Indeed he did," Alex said. "And I am really thrilled—for Maria."

"Huh?" J.R. climbed onto one of the stools behind the counter while Alex kept standing. He set down the book next to the paper he had been writing on, which J.R. saw was a note card with the name Kate written on the envelope.

"Maria is going to take over June's, although I'll still own the place. It took me a while to know what I wanted, but I've figured out what it is and Ava's dad finally agreed to extend the lease. As you know, once I set my mind to something, I've got a way with words." Alex winked. "But in those months of negotiating, I was torn about what to do. I love June's, and it's a special place for me. But I realized I also wanted to try something new, and I was scared to do it. I was focused on the lease, a big, outside force that I couldn't really control, but what I needed to focus on was my own decision. It took me a while, but I decided to take the plunge."

"Plunge into what?" J.R. asked. Whatever it was sounded exciting, but she hoped Alex wasn't going too far.

"I'm going back to school to become a teacher. Maria's going to take over the day-to-day at June's, although we'll need to hire her some help, and maybe even get her an intern if anyone you know is interested."

"I love that idea," J.R. said, meaning Alex's change of profession but also the thought of spending more time at June's. "Is Ms. Kline going to share her magazines with you?"

"Nope, and nor would I ask her to. It takes someone with

a certain wanderlust to be in charge of the magazines." J.R. smiled to hear Alex mention wanderlust, just like her dad had done at the beginning of the year. "I like to stick closer to home. First, I'm going to Teachers College up in Morningside Heights." J.R. remembered the name from the letter of recommendation on Ms. Kline's desk. "Then I'll look for a position right here in New York City, maybe even at the same school where Eleanor taught me."

"I think you'll be a great teacher," J.R. said. "But that doesn't seem like it's a note to end on. It's a new beginning!" Alex didn't say anything at all or even acknowledge her compliment. That's when it dawned on her—Alex hadn't been referring to June's or himself. He had been talking about J.R. "My turn's over." She could barely look at Alex as she said it.

Alex nodded sympathetically. "Kate coaxed it out of you. She's a truly special teacher like Eleanor that way. But more importantly, J.R., you did it."

"But I can't be done!" J.R. protested. She remembered the rush of writing a story and seeing it come to life. It wasn't fair to have to give up that amazing power. "How am I supposed to go back to normal?"

"Will you, though?" Alex asked.

"Without the magazines? Of course!"

"Without the magazines, yes, things will be different. But I don't think you'll ever revert to quite the same person you used to be. Do you?"

J.R. looked at Alex and then at George, who had jumped

onto the counter and offered a friendly kiss for the first time. J.R. didn't need to say anything, really. They both knew the answer was no. But staying silent was hardly the spirit of everything she had learned. "No," she said. "The magazines changed me."

Chapter 31

ON THE LAST TUESDAY MORNING of school before winter break, the sixth-grade parents came to Nic for the sea shanty assembly, where both homerooms performed for the entire middle school. It was really a cross-curriculum effort. The ocean mural from art hung behind them, and they complemented their singing with moves they had practiced in dance class, like pulling together on imaginary ropes and climbing the cargo net at the back of the gym with the PE teachers standing below as spotters. Everyone wore a white shirt, with an assortment of bandannas, eye patches, and gold hoops of their choosing. It was loud, and fun, and the whole room was packed with people ready for vacation.

After the show, Ms. Kline welcomed kids and parents back to her classroom for snacks. J.R. gave her mom and dad a tour, moving quickly through the wall of illustrated longships and lingering over the ceiling, where her dad wanted to identify every constellation he could find. As that got boring, Ms. Kline appeared with a tray of Munchkins.

"That was fantastic," J.R.'s mom said, equally relieved to be interrupted by the teacher.

"I agree. The class did a lovely job." True to form, Ms. Kline barely smiled. But she also fought what must have been her instinct to intercede as Curtis walked by leading several boys in a round of "What Shall We Do with a Drunken Sailor," which was definitely not part of their official sea shanty repertoire.

"What are your plans for the winter vacation?" J.R.'s father asked as he took two little doughnuts and popped one into his mouth.

"Actually, I have some news." Ms. Kline looked around for an open spot and, not seeing anything better, put the doughnut tray down on Curtis's desk. Guided by a sixth sense, the marauding band of boys descended on the sweets. "I'll be moving to New Orleans."

"What?" Luckily, J.R. hadn't taken a Munchkin or she would have spat it out. It hadn't occurred to her that her teacher would leave so soon, even if she was bound to be summoned away to help another student.

"You're leaving in the middle of the school year?" J.R.'s dad made no effort to hide his annoyance. Anything dreamy about wanderlust was not on his mind.

"Unfortunately, I'm needed elsewhere. But we've done a lot

of good work, and I know the students will continue to thrive, your daughter included."

It was clear that J.R.'s dad wanted to say something else, probably that Ms. Kline shouldn't bounce from school to school so much. "Ms. Kline's right," J.R. said before he could get started. "We did a lot of interesting projects already, and she's taught me how to keep going on my own." J.R. meant it, more than her father knew. She was acutely aware, though, that one *Gothamite* assignment was yet to complete its full cycle: J.R.'s haiku. No results had materialized. "What about us, Dad?" she added. "What are we doing for winter break? Maybe getting a puppy?"

Her dad scowled, but with a smile behind his eyes. "Well, your mother asked me about that, actually. And we agreed to talk about it all together. You'll have to convince us it's the right thing to do, though. And you'll have to walk the dog when it snows." J.R.'s father glanced out the window, where the sky was a flat, white color that suggested winter weather was coming.

This, J.R. thought, was definitely progress, and she was confident she could make her case.

"Can we borrow J.R. for a second?" Violet interrupted their conversation along with Ava, whose parents were talking to Aria and her mom in the corner. Seeing them reminded J.R. that she also needed to talk to her parents about Aria's French camp idea, and maybe about finding her own sleepaway camp for later in the summer. She hadn't even told Aria that she really did want to go, which J.R. felt bad about. There was definitely no shortage of things for the Silvers to discuss over winter break, and she would talk to Aria as soon as they did.

"You're not leaving yet, right?" J.R. asked her teacher. Of course Ms. Kline wouldn't be walking out right then, but the question popped into J.R.'s mind and right out of her mouth.

"No, not yet. We've got the rest of the week to say goodbye. And I'll be sure you know where to find me."

That was the reassurance J.R. needed to hear. She followed Violet and Ava toward the windows and explained Ms. Kline's impending departure along the way.

"Violet doesn't have a date for the dance on Friday," Ava said. J.R. immediately bristled. Was she really bringing up that sore subject now? "I was going to go with Curtis, but we decided to make it a girls' night instead. Aria's in, too, although Adelaide's sticking with Matt." Ava rolled her eyes. "Do you want to join us? It could be a quadruple date."

"We're going to sleep over at Ava's apartment afterward, Adelaide included," Violet added before J.R. gave her a quizzical look. "I know, I know. But if she wants Matt, she can have him. I'm over it. Our girls' night will be much better, anyway." Violet and Ava both laughed.

J.R. was glad to be invited. Truly. She waited a second, nervous about what she wanted to do and about what Violet's reaction would be. Despite acting like she had moved on, J.R. was pretty sure that Violet's feelings about Matt were still raw, and J.R. was determined to be a good friend. Still, she thought Violet would understand. "The sleepover sounds so fun," she said. "Thanks for the invitation. I think I might ask Tommy to be my date for the dance part, though."

Immediately, Violet grinned. "I like that idea," she said. "I like it a lot."

Seizing on her momentum, J.R. headed toward the snack table, where Tommy was eating a doughnut. She thought about Claudia Kincaid from the *Mixed-Up Files*, and how Claudia is desperate to become different. J.R. never felt that urgency, but it did feel good to think about how much had changed. She had lots of things to say, and now she was better at saying them. She had good friends, and she was pretty sure she'd make more. She could be bold and be forgiving. At the desk beside her, J.R. noticed something red on top of a silver napkin sprinkled with doughnut crumbs. She shivered but then called quietly to Nathalie and inclined her head.

"Thanks!" Nathalie said as she grabbed her retainer just before Curtis walked by. He almost certainly would have been ready with a cutting comment if he had seen the device first.

The world felt right.

J.R. took one last look around the room before she talked to Tommy. She made eye contact with Violet, who held up her hand and curled her finger. J.R. inhaled deeply, and then she curled back.

Author's Note

J.R. Silver Writes Her World emerged from my own fourth-grade class. Our teacher, whom I'll call Ms. K, had a collection of *New Yorker* magazine covers that she used as prompts for creative writing assignments. Like the fictional *Gothamite*, each *New Yorker* cover is truly a work of art. I looked back at decades of them for inspiration when writing this book—they range from pastoral to provocative, and a lot of times they're funny. While the *Gothamite* covers from Ms. Kline's collection are all the product of my imagination, I hope some of them will speak to you as many *New Yorker* covers speak to me.

The Metropolitan Museum of Art

One of the things I most enjoyed about creating this novel was wandering around the Metropolitan Museum of Art looking for artworks and galleries to incorporate into the story. Each piece featured in *J.R. Silver* is real, although it might not always be on display. The Met doesn't allow sleepovers, but you can try to re-create J.R.'s story during the day. Don't worry if you can't visit in person, because you can learn a lot about the museum and the collection at metmuseum.org.

From the Mixed-Up Files of Mrs. Basil E. Frankweiler

I adore New York City, and one of my favorite books set in New York is *From the Mixed-Up Files of Mrs. Basil E. Frankweiler* by E. L. Konigsburg. It's about Claudia and Jamie Kincaid, a brother and sister who run away to the Met, and about Claudia's desire to go home a new person, improved by her adventure. The path she sees to improvement is to solve a high-profile mystery: whether a statue the museum acquired was sculpted, in fact, by the famous Renaissance artist Michelangelo Buonarroti. You'll have to read the book to find out how her adventure unfolds.

The Cultural Services of the French Embassy

Several years ago, a friend took me to Albertine, a French and English bookstore inside the Payne Whitney Mansion on Fifth Avenue. The ornate turn-of-the-century building is home to the Cultural Services of the French Embassy. Late in the process of writing this book, I learned that in the mid-1990s, a professor attending an event in the building encountered a sculpture of Cupid that had stood in the lobby from the time it was a private home. She realized that the sculpture was truly special: It was one of the earliest works of Michelangelo, but no one knew. Today, the sculpture is on loan to the Met, and a replica stands in the mansion.

Acknowledgments

I will be forever grateful to my wonderful agent, Jennifer Unter. I couldn't be happier for us to be a team.

I owe unending thanks to my publisher Christy Ottaviano and my editor Jessica Anderson. Christy saw a spark in *J.R. Silver* and patiently nurtured the story into this novel. Jessica immediately grasped what I was trying to do and time and again (and again) pointed me toward more meaningful ways to do it. What a dream and a joy to work with them both.

Thank you also to production editor Jake Regier and designer Jenny Kimura for their thoughtful collaboration and many talents, and to Bill Grace, Andie Divelbiss, Mara Brashem, Shivani Annirood, and Christie Michel for their creativity and efforts getting this book into the hands of readers. A hearty thanks to Chelen Écija, too, whose illustrations make me smile from the cover to the last page.

Catherine Frank's early guidance put me on this path.

I owe an enormous debt of gratitude to my many creative teachers. Ms. K's fourth-grade classroom sparked the idea for this book.

Friends and family shared their loyalty, curiosity, inspiration, and much-needed humor as I started writing and began to share that writing with the world. Thank you!

I can't believe my luck in having the parents and sister I do. We had a lot of fun together when I was J.R.'s age, and that's even more true now that we're folding in the next generation.

My husband, Fred, is my rock. I would not have written this book, or anything like it, without him.

Lily, Emilia, and Charlotte inspire me. I love you, I love you, I love you. Never stop reading!

FW Dassori

MELISSA DASSORI

lives in New York City with her husband
and three daughters, with whom she especially likes to share books, spend time outside, eat ice cream, and travel. *J.R. Silver
Writes Her World* is her first novel.

Melissa invites you to visit her at
melissadassori.com.